The Tombstone Vendetta

When Billy Clanton and his friends are murdered in Tombstone by the town marshal and his deputies, the growing tension between the local authorities and the ranchers spirals out of control.

The once sleepy frontier town is mired in hatred, with bad blood and scores to settle on both sides. Families are torn asunder as the violence rages on. Will there ever be peace in Tombstone? Or will peace only come when one side reigns victorious?

The Tombstone Vendetta

Ralph Hayes

A Black Horse Western

ROBERT HALE · LONDON

© Ralph Hayes 2010
First published in Great Britain 2010

ISBN 978-0-7090-8866-0

Robert Hale Limited
Clerkenwell House
Clerkenwell Green
London EC1R 0HT

www.halebooks.com

Typeset by
Derek Doyle & Associates, Shaw Heath
Printed and bound in Great Britain by
CPI Antony Rowe, Chippenham and Eastbourne

CHAPTER ONE

The grim funeral procession passed solemnly down the length of Allen Street with grave decorum, only the creaking of wagon wheels and muffled hoofbeats breaking the silence of that cool October afternoon. Isaac 'Ike' Clanton and a McLaury widow rode side by side on a buckboard wagon situated in the lead of a hearse and two coffin wagons. On each of those wagons was situated a silver-trimmed, black-painted pine casket. Billy Clanton, Ike's brother, was visible inside the hearse, and on the wagons open caskets revealed the bodies of Tom and Frank McLaury, exposed to the view of bystanders who lined the street on both sides. The faces of the corpses were sunken and pallid, because local undertaker Ream had no make-up kit to improve their appearance. He had laid silver quarters on their eyes, and would add that expense to the fee for the funerals. On the bed of the lead wagon bearing Ike and the widow, a cowboy stood holding up a handwritten sign that read, MURDERED IN THE STREETS OF TOMBSTONE.

Most of the faces in the crowd along the street were somber in acknowlegment of the tragedy of yet three more seemingly avoidable deaths that had occurred in their small frontier town. A few faces reflected tension and fear, because the three deaths hadn't appeared to resolve anything in the growing conflict between local authority and the surrounding ranchers, and could be the beginning of something quite terrible.

As the entourage kicked up dust passing the Cosmopolitan Hotel, the wagons creaking and groaning under the weight of their cargo, the cowboy with the sign glared up toward a balcony where three men in black suits sat on hard chairs and watched the procession. They were Morgan, Virgil and Wyatt Earp. They, and a dentist named Doc Holliday, had killed the three men in the funeral procession at the OK Corral two days previously. Virgil was the town marshal, and Morgan and Wyatt were his deputies.

'Filthy murderers!' the man with the sign yelled up at them. 'This ain't over!'

The wagons rumbled on down the street, and a few of the cowboys following it glanced up at the men in black and grinned, then rode on toward the cemetery. Virgil Earp, a large, beefy man with a round face and mustache, turned toward Wyatt, on his left. Virgil had been shot in the right calf at the shoot-out, and limped on the leg.

'Did you see them looks the cowboys give us?' His voice was deep and booming, and his manner intimidating. 'This ain't going away, Wyatt.'

Wyatt Earp ran a hand through his dark hair. He had tipped his chair back against the wall behind them. He was a fine-looking fellow, with a long handlebar mustache and ruminative, steely eyes. His face was aquiline, and women considered him handsome. He was always calm, cool and poised, emitting an aura of confidence and strength. He was deadly with a gun, and few cared to challenge him. He had been a law enforcement officer previously in Dodge City, but was also wanted for horse-theft and robbery from his early, wild days. He had deferred to Virgil for the top law enforcement job here in Tombstone, but he was the acknowledged leader of the brothers.

'I know that.' He looked down the dusty street, past the haphazard collection of weathered clapboard buildings lining it, hemmed in on all sides by canvas-and-board shanties and tents. 'Ike won't even remember those coffins going into the ground. He's crazy in the head now about Billy. You saw, he couldn't even glance up here as he passed. I reckon he's plotting a payback for Billy in his head right now. He won't be satisfied till all the Earp brothers are dead and buried like Billy.'

'That's fine,' Morgan said rather loudly. The funeral procession was now passing out of sight down the street. 'I feel the by-God same. I won't rest easy till all of them Clantons have earned their just deserts.' He was slim with an angular, bony face, and wore a mustache like his brothers. He presented an almost perpetual frown when things weren't going to his liking. Of the three, he was the aggressive hot-head.

Morgan rubbed gently at his side, where he had been shot shallowly at the corral. He still wore a thick bandage there. Big Virgil had been nicked in the calf, and that was causing his slight limp. Wyatt had escaped injury.

Virgil grunted. 'Well, remember, Morgan. I'm the town marshal here. We represent the law. We're not a bunch of vigilantes. If we're patient, we'll catch the Clantons red-handed in the act of rustling or robbery. The governor and even the federal authorities have said the territory has to be rid of these marauding cowboys. They stand behind us, as long as we use the law right to do our work. It's only

7

our local sheriff that stands with the Clantons.'

'Johnny Behan has a lot of influence here,' Wyatt reminded them. 'He plays cards with Mayor Clum and Judge Wells Spicer. And he'll back just about any play Ike would decide to make against us.'

'If you run against him in November, you might beat him out of that badge,' Morgan said morosely. 'Then we'd have all the lawing jobs under our control here, and could operate with a free hand.'

'That won't happen,' Wyatt said quietly. 'The cowboys are in the majority, and can control any election. Now that we've taken a stand against the Clantons, they'd never let me win another office. Even the ones working on other ranches. The corral shoot-out will unite them.'

Morgan leaned forward to look over at Wyatt. He rode as a shotgun messenger for Wells, Fargo as his regular job, and was deputized by Virgil only when needed. At the moment, he was still wearing a badge on his black vest, like Wyatt and Virgil. When they were out on the street in this cool weather, they all wore black frock-coats over their 'artillery'. They also all wore starched white shirts and lariat ties, making them look more like businessmen from Kansas City than lawmen. The rough-hewn cowboys laughed behind their backs at their garb.

'Well, I'm for ending the Clantons' reign of terror as much as anyone,' Morgan offered. 'But I don't want to take a year to do it. We didn't come here to clean up the West, Wyatt. At least, I didn't. I thought we came out here to invest our money and get rich. We've got our cash into the poolhall, and the Oriental saloon. If we drag this out very long, the cowboys will stop patronizing those places, because of us. Then we might as well pack up our bags and ride out.'

Wyatt gave him a sober look. 'I kind of like this place, Morgan. There's room for growth out here. Providing there's some law and order. We can make a big difference here in Tombstone. Be patient, brother. We're in a fight here, and it won't be over in a week.'

'Well, Clanton will come after us now, for sure. We killed Billy. And the McLaurys are his close friends. We should hit them before they come for us.'

'We don't have any legal justification, Morgan,' Virgil reasoned with him. 'Just keep a low profile for a while, till this corral fight blows over. They'll make a mistake one of these days. Then we'll take them down.'

'I'm not lying low for anybody, let alone a nest of snakes like the Clantons and McLaurys!' Morgan told him hotly.

Wyatt shook his head slowly. 'All right, Morgan. We'll talk about this later. I'm going inside to join James and the womenfolk. Anybody care to join me?'

But before either of them could respond, the screen door behind them opened and Wyatt's wife Mattie came out onto the balcony outside Wyatt's rooms. She was a petite, pretty girl with dark hair and lovely eyes. 'Wyatt. You've got company.'

The men all turned toward her quizzically. 'Company?' Virgil said.

'It's Sheriff Behan,' Mattie said. 'Just back from the cemetery.'

Virgil and Wyatt exchanged a sober look, then all three men rose and accompanied Mattie inside. Wyatt rented a two-room suite, and the room they entered was the parlor, with a long sofa, easy chairs and a desk on a side wall. The bedroom was off to the right, through a closed door.

Virgil's wife Allie and Morgan's wife Louisa sat at a card table across the room, where they and Mattie had been

9

playing pinochle. James, the eldest of the Earp brothers, stood glaring at the new visitor, Sheriff John Behan and his deputy Frank Stilwell.

'Our honorable sheriff wants to see you boys,' James said acidly. He was slim, like Morgan, and had receding hair. He had never been involved in lawing, and had come to Tombstone with his brothers to tend bar. He had recently fulfilled his hopes of becoming a saloon owner and had become the proprietor of the Sampling Room saloon.

Behan nodded his head toward the other Earps genially. 'Wyatt. Boys. I hope I'm not interrupting anything important.' He was a slim, good-looking young man, dressed much like the Earps. He always kept on the good side of the ranchers because he respected their voting power, and had immediately seen the Earps as a challenge to his authority in the area. 'I think you all know my deputy, Frank Stilwell.'

Wyatt nodded. 'Frank.' He waved a hand toward the women. 'I don't think you've met our wives. That sassy-looking one over there is Mattie, she belongs to me.'

Mattie gave him a mock frown.

'Those other two are Louisa and Allie. They see to it that Morgan and Virgil get their shirts buttoned straight in the morning.'

'Right.' Allie grinned. 'Virgil would sleep in his boots some nights if I didn't pull them off.'

Big Virgil cast an acid look her way, and the grin slid off her face. She was a large, outspoken woman who had tried to dissuade Virgil from coming to Tombstone with Wyatt and Morgan.

Stilwell was enjoying it. 'That's a good one! The marshal has to be undressed by his wife!' He was always speaking when he should have been silent.

All three brothers regarded him somberly. Behan cleared his throat and glanced toward his deputy. 'That's enough, Frank.'

'Can I offer you a cup of coffee, Sheriff?' Wyatt said after some moments.

'No, we won't be here long,' Behan said. He had removed his Stetson and was now crimping its brim between his hands. 'We're here on business, Wyatt.'

'What kind of business?' Virgil boomed out hostilely.

Wyatt turned to him. 'Let the man talk, Marshal.'

Behan took a deep breath. 'Well, you see, it's this way. Witnesses have come forward who say you boys provoked the shoot-out two days ago, and then gunned them men down in cold blood.'

A heavy, cold silence settled into the room. After a long moment, Morgan fairly yelled a reply. 'That's a lie, Behan, and you know it! You were there!'

'I wasn't right at the corral,' the sheriff replied. 'Anyway, it's not up to me. Charges have been made by the Clantons, and the court has to listen to them. The town council is in this, too. Judge Spicer says you have to answer the charges, Wyatt. You and Holliday. So far they don't want you, Virgil, or Morgan.'

Mattie stood up from the card table quickly. 'You've got your nerve, Behan! Do you do anything the Clantons tell you?'

'Now, now, Mattie,' Wyatt said smoothly. 'The sheriff here is just trying to do his job. Just who are these witnesses, Sheriff?'

'I'm not at liberty to say just now,' Behan replied, his mouth dry. 'That will all be made known to you later. Anyway, I have to place you under arrest for now. We're going to go pick up Doc next, and we hoped you'd help us bring him in peaceful.'

Beefy Virgil came and stood nose to nose with Behan. 'You're bought and paid for, Behan! And you don't have the authority to arrest a deputy town marshal! Your jurisdiction lies outside the city!'

'Not if there's malfeasance of office in the marshal's ranks,' Behan replied, looking very nervous now.

'Malfeasance!' Virgil yelled. 'Ike and Billy Clanton threatened my deputies with violence, and then refused to disarm themselves! We went down to Fremont Street just to take their guns. Then they challenged us again. We are the law inside these town boundaries, Behan! The cowboys were making a mockery of it!'

'Well, the witnesses say you boys fired without warning,' Behan said weakly. 'This isn't something I can decide, Virgil. You know that. The law has to take its course.'

'And don't you just like that!' red-faced Morgan yelled at him.

Behan shook his head. 'I've said what I had to say. Now I have to ask you to accompany us down to my office, Wyatt. And we'd like to get Doc along the way.'

'Doc will kill you if you try to arrest him,' Virgil said easily, in his deep voice.

Morgan drew a Colt revolver from a belt holster. 'Wyatt isn't going anywhere, Behan!'

Wyatt put a hand on Morgan's arm. 'Put it away, Morgan.'

Morgan eyed him with a deep frown. 'What?'

'John here is the sheriff of Cochise County,' Wyatt said in a quiet, calm voice. 'I'll take a walk down the street with him. We'll get this all cleared up. I'll stop by Doc's room with you, too, Sheriff. So he won't shoot you.'

'Don't go with them, Wyatt!' Mattie said loudly as Morgan holstered his sidearm grudgingly.

'Stop this, Virgil!' Allie called out.

Louisa, Morgan's wife, was crying. James had been quiet all this time. He walked over and put an arm around Louisa's shoulder. 'You're upsetting the women, Sheriff. Couldn't you have done this in a more civilized manner?' He was the oldest, and most passive of the four brothers. He had always been more like their fifth brother Warren, who still lived in California, running a business there.

'You ain't involved in this, saloon boy,' Stilwell said.

Wyatt grew a frown. 'If you can't keep that nitwit quiet, Sheriff, I might have to do something about him,' he said in a hard, even tone.

Stilwell's face went winch-wire tight. 'Now just a minute here.'

Behan turned to him fiercely. 'Get on down to the office, Frank, and get them papers ready for us!'

'Huh?'

'Now!' Behan said loudly.

Frank slid a hand across his mouth. 'Well. I'll go get the papers ready for them two to sign then.' He looked around the room uncertainly, then turned and left.

'I apologize for Frank's rudeness, Wyatt,' Behan said softly. 'I reckon he was weaned too soon.'

'That will do it in some men,' Wyatt agreed. 'Well, let's get this over with, Sheriff.'

Mattie came over and grabbed Wyatt's arm. 'Will you be back here tonight?'

'He better be!' Morgan growled.

Wyatt turned to his wife. 'Don't worry your head, darling.' Mattie's eyes were tearing, too, now. Her life was not a good one with Wyatt. When he wasn't in danger

13

because of his Peacemaker, he might be out all night with some dance-hall girl. But she had had a checkered past, herself. 'This will all be over before you know it.'

A couple of minutes later he and Virgil left with Behan. On the way to the sheriff's office, they all stopped at a rooming-house down the street, where Wyatt told Doc they had to go with Behan, under arrest. Holliday stared at Wyatt for a moment as if he had lost his mind.

'Is this a joke, Wyatt?' He looked a little like Morgan Earp, but was thinner, and emaciated-looking, his cheek-bones sunk in on themselves, his eyes rheumy-looking. But he was a dangerous man with a gun. He was tubercular, and slowly dying, and seemed to welcome the challenge of a gunfight as if he had nothing to lose.

After a mild persuasion by Wyatt, though, he left peaceably with them. Like Morgan, he had sustained only a grazing wound at the OK Corral, but was feeling the wound more than Morgan. He grimaced as he rose from a straight chair and pulled a coat on, with his landmark white-silk scarf at his neck.

'You're lucky you came with Wyatt, Johnny.' He grinned a thin, bony grin as they all left the room together. 'The county might have had to appoint another sheriff come morning.'

Behan didn't reply. He didn't want to antagonize either of his detainees.

The arrests of Wyatt and Doc were official less than a half-hour later, and then followed a potentially explosive moment. Behan knew the people behind the accusations would expect an incarceration, so he persuaded the two to spend one night in a holding cell behind his office with the promise of a steak dinner there prepared by his own wife, Victoria. Behan also brought a bottle of aged wine, and Wyatt and Doc played cards for most of the night.

They were arraigned before Judge Wells Spicer the following morning, with Ike and Phin Clanton present, along with the Earp brothers. Wyatt and Doc were represented by a fellow named Thomas Fitch, a local attorney, and Cochise County brought in the attorney Lyttleton Price to prosecute. Ike Clanton's personal lawyer was Ben Goodrich. The accused moved for a dismissal, alleging the charges were groundless, but Spicer rejected the plea. They then plead not guilty to murder and a date was set for a preliminary hearing.

There was no panic in the Earp camp, and Doc Holliday treated it all as a great joke. When the hearing finally began, the courtroom and street were filled with supporters, detractors, and the just plain curious. In the first days, the Clantons brought on three cowboy witnesses who claimed to have seen the plain murder of Billy Clanton, and Tom and Frank McLaury, but it was apparent they had been coached by Ike, and had seen next to nothing. Later in the long hearing Wyatt and Doc testified.

'Now, isn't it true that you arrived on Fremont Street with the express purpose of killing your hated enemies there, that is, the Clantons and McLaurys?' the somber prosecutor put to Doc on cross-examination.

'I arrived there hoping nobody shot my belt buckle off, because my long johns underwear was being laundered!' Doc retorted.

There was a loud burst of laughter from the spectators, and Judge Spicer had to gavel the room to order. 'All right, that's enough hilarity,' he shouted at the crowd. 'Keep it quiet or I'll clear the courtroom!'

15

After a moment, the next question was hurled at Doc. 'You've heard witnesses testify that you and Wyatt Earp drew down on these ranchers without warning, and shot them down in cold blood. How do you answer these charges?'

'Well, my idea is, it must be hard to see what's going on at Fremont Street when you're down at the Oriental throwing down shots of Planter's Rye,' Doc rejoined caustically.

More laughter, but more subdued. Doc was making the lawyer look bad.

'Your honor, I ask the court to demand that the defendant's answers be responsive to the questions put to him.'

Spicer thought about that for a moment. He turned to Doc. 'Do you have reason to believe that the county's witnesses were elsewhere at the time of the shoot-out, Dr Holliday?'

'I have reason to believe those scoundrels are in there bending their elbows every chance they get,' Doc responded.

There was another ripple of laughter from the assemblage, and Spicer gaveled the room to order again.

'All right, Doctor. I get your point. Counsel, do you have anything further for this defendant?'

'No, your honor. He appears unable to add anything significant to the evidence.'

'Then, Mr Fitch, you may call your next witness.'

Fitch rose. 'The defense calls Assistant Marshal Wyatt Earp to the stand.'

A quiet murmuring among the onlookers.

Wyatt rose from the table looking like an official from the territorial capital, in his dark suit, starched shirt and slicked-back hair. An expectant hush fell over the crowd as he went through a small gate and stood at the witness chair beside the judge's bench. The court stenographer administered an oath, and Wyatt seated himself on the chair.

All the Earps and their wives were lined up along the first row behind the barrier. Mattie looked very tense, but gave Wyatt a big smile. Virgil sat forward on his seat, looking very much like a heavyweight boxer waiting for the next round of a big fight.

Wyatt was asked to identify himself, and then Fitch leaned on the handrail beside the witness chair. 'Now, Mr Earp. You're the assistant city marshal here in Tombstone, is that correct?'

Wyatt nodded, sitting ramrod-erect on the chair. He had been relieved of his Colt Peacemaker revolvers but his presence in the witness chair was formidable to those in the big room who considered him their enemy.

'That's right, Counsel.'

'How long have you held that position?'

'Almost from the moment I arrived here, some months ago.'

'Are you familiar with the Clantons and McLaurys?'

Wyatt ran a hand through his handlebar mustache. 'I've met about all of them at one time or another, I guess.'

'Have you dealt with them in an official capacity as a law enforcement officer of this city?'

'Yes, I have. A while back the McLaurys stole some mules from the cavalry post nearby, and I went out to the ranch and repossessed the animals, with Virgil and Morgan. We were going to arrest Frank McLaury and Ike Clanton, but the Army dropped charges. The Clanton and McLaury brothers have also been suspects in cattle-rustling events in some Southern counties.'

'Objection!' the prosecutor protested.

'Sustained,' Spicer ruled.

Wyatt's lawyer sighed. 'Had any of the Clantons or McLaurys threatened you personally, Mr Earp?'

'The Clantons have hated us ever since we arrived here,' Wyatt said. 'Before we arrived, they did as they wanted. There was no law officer here to rein them in, then we arrived. Yes, they've threatened every one of us.'

Behan, sitting in the second row of spectators, stood up red-faced. 'I object to that remark! We had the sheriff's department here long before your arrival, Wyatt! We always co-operated with the previous marshal to keep the peace in Tombstone!'

'Tell that to the ranchers who had their cattle stolen!' big Virgil Earp called back.

There was chaos in the room. Judge Spicer banged his gavel over and over and eventually silence settled in again. He scowled at the crowd.

'If you people want to stay for the rest of this, I warn you! There will be no more outbursts like that one!'

After a few moments, Thomas Fitch resumed. 'Did or did not the Clantons invite your brothers to a showdown on Fremont Street, in front of the OK Corral?'

'They did.'

'And did you go there to kill them?'

'We went there to arrest them. They had been abusing their privilege of carrying firearms in the city. It was going to be a minor thing.'

'What happened when you got there?'

'Billy Clanton and Frank McLaury cocked their revolvers in their holsters. I told them to hold it, and I wanted their guns. Then they both drew and opened fire.

Myself, Virgil, Morgan and Doc Holliday all returned fire, with Tom McLaury joining in against us. Doc, Virgil and Morgan were all hit but not fatally. Billy Clanton, Frank McLaury and Tom McLaury died of their wounds. It was all over and done in just seconds.'

'You're a liar!' Ike Clanton shouted from the crowd. He had testified earlier, saying the Earps had fired first, and without warning. 'You're a murdering liar, Earp!'

Wyatt cast a cool look on him, while Judge Spicer pounded again with the gavel. 'Order in the court! I mean it, I'll send every mother's son of you home!'

The state's prosecutor wasn't really able to challenge Wyatt's testimony, and by end of the day his part in the proceeding was finished. A few days later, after Virgil and Morgan had substantiated Wyatt's version of events, the mini-trial was concluded. And since this was technically a preliminary inquiry, the decision was entirely in Spicer's hands. After a brief adjournment, he resumed the hearing once more. The stenographer took a seat beside the bench, and a big, armed bailiff took a stance against a nearby wall.

The spectators were excited but quiet, with Ike and Phin Clanton and a whole cadre of cowpokes from the ranch now usurping most of the up-front seats. The courtroom was small and airless, and a quiet utterance could be heard distinctly in any corner of the room.

Wyatt and Doc sat at the defense counsel table with Fitch, and the other Earps shared front seats with Ike's people. The beefy prosecutor sat grim-faced at the other counsel table. Judge Spicer waited until the room was perfectly quiet.

'All right, folks. I know you've all been waiting a long while for a conclusion to this very confusing case, and I'm prepared now to render my decision.'

Wyatt, Doc, and Fitch all sat expectantly but calmly, Doc leaning on his silver-tipped cane and looking very much like an undertaker. Under his shirt, his wound was bleeding slightly through his bandage.

'I've given this a lot of thought,' Spicer began. 'And I've taken into account the bad blood between the defendants and the ranchers who mourn the deceased individuals in this case. We have so many versions of this violent incident that the true facts may never be known. But it must be remembered that the burden of proof in this trial, as in any other, rests with the county. Also, guilt must be established beyond the shadow of a doubt. In this case, that hasn't happened.'

There was a big uproar from the Clantons and their cowboy friends, and Spicer waited for the noise to subside.

'I'll put it short and simple,' Spicer finally continued. 'John Holliday was duly deputized by Virgil Earp before the action, so all of these men were officers of the law charged with the duty of arresting and disarming brave and determined men who were experts in the use of firearms, as quick as thought and as certain as death, and who had previously declared their intentions not to be arrested nor disarmed. Therefore, I find the defendants' actions as presented here to be within the authority of the law, and they are exonerated of the crime of murder.'

'Are you crazy, Spicer!' Ike Clanton shouted angrily, rising to his feet.

'Do you call this justice?' a cowboy yelled from a back row. His name was Pony Deal, and he had been hired by Ike Clanton because he was good with a gun. He was a ranch foreman, and had been on a number of rustling raids under Ike's orders.

'We don't need you, Spicer!' another cowpoke called out. 'We got our own court of justice!'

'Bailiff, remove that man,' Spicer said grimly.

The bailiff moved to the rear, but before he could physically remove the offender the fellow left, shouting invectives to a crowd outside. Spicer shook his head, and went on.

'I'm not finished. In my judgment, Marshal Virgil Earp commited an injudicious and censurable act in calling on his brothers and Dr Holliday to go disarm the Clantons and McLaurys. This could be considered unnecessary force, and inflammatory to the other side. But when we consider the conditions of affairs incidental to a frontier community; the lawlessness and disregard for human life, the existence of a law-defying element in our midst, and the feeling of fear that has existed here because of the perceived prevalence of bad, desperate, and reckless men who have terrorized the county, along with the many threats that have been made against the Earps, I can find no criminality in Virgil Earp's unwise act. This case is herewith dismissed on grounds of lack of evidence.'

There were a few cheers in the big room from townsfolk, but there was a much more vociferous outburst from the many ranchers and cowboys from the Clanton and McLaury clans. As Judge Spicer rose and hurriedly left the room through a side door, there were shouts of anger again from those present.

'Death of justice!' one lanky cowboy yelled out.

'Now you can deal with us!' another one shouted.

Wyatt and Doc rose from their seats and turned to regard the shouters quietly. The wives were staring angrily toward the noise-makers.

'You boys won't last out the week!' some hot-head called out.

'Now you answer to our justice!' another one chimed in.

The cowboy named Pony Deal worked his way up to the front, and leaned forward past Ike Clanton to speak softly now to the Earps. 'You better watch your backs, boys. We ain't forgetting what you done!'

'Another word from you, Pony, and I'll throw your butt in jail,' Virgil said easily to him.

Deal just laughed a guttural laugh, and he and the Clantons began making their way out of the building, with Ike turning twice to glare at Wyatt. Sheriff Behan and his man Breakenridge then came forward to speak with the defendants.

'You and Doc better get yourselves home, Wyatt,' Behan told them. 'The mood around here is pretty grim.'

'Wyatt don't run from nobody, Behan!' the fiery Morgan spoke up.

Mattie came and put an arm on Wyatt's. 'Come on, Deputy. You've had enough excitement for one day. I've got a nice stew waiting for all of us at the hotel. We'll have us a celebration.'

Wyatt regarded her with a half-smile. He knew there was little to celebrate. Their defeat of the criminal suit had only inflamed the Clantons even more than they had been. And there was an overlying stench of vengeance in the air, like a night fog off the nearby swamp outside town.

He nodded to his wife. 'Sure,' he said quietly. 'We'll have us a party.'

Then they all left the building in solemn silence.

CHAPTER TWO

Things were very quiet in Tombstone for the next several weeks. Even the Saturday nights were quieter on Allen Street. At the Oriental saloon, where Wyatt had his money invested and where James worked as bartender, business fell off to a trickle. The Clanton cowpokes decided they wouldn't be served at a bar by James, or pour their hard-earned cash into profit for Wyatt.

But it was more than that. Something was brewing. The McLaurys were now so afraid of the Earps that they lost interest in carrying the feud any farther, but the Clantons, under Ike's leadership now that the old man was dead, were in a deadly mood. They had been surprised and irritated when Mayor Clum had brought Virgil Earp in as town marshal upon the death of the previous lawman. That fellow had taken no interest in the lawlessness of the ranchers, and they had Sheriff Behan bought and paid for. Then Virgil Earp moved in with three brothers, deputized two of them, and announced his intention to clean up the town. Firearms couldn't be worn inside the city, and lawbreakers would be prosecuted. All of this made the Clantons angry, and worried that these newcomers would also try to abort their profitable raids on Mexican ranches in the southern part of the territory. And now, the Earps had killed a Clanton, and to kill a Clanton in Cochise County was a mortal sin.

Virgil Earp's hotel room was adjacent to Wyatt's at the hotel, and the entire family met there one dark night about a month after the acquittal. Doc Holliday had been invited to the meeting, but had declined due to one of his regular attacks from his worsening tuberculosis. It was the wives of the brothers who had insisted on a sit-down talk, and Wyatt's Mattie began the discussion. She and the other two wives were sitting together on a long sofa across the big room from a double bed. The men, including James, were scattered around the room, three on chairs and Virgil propped against his headboard.

'I realize you boys just want to ignore what's happened here,' Mattie began. 'Like it doesn't mean anything. But it does. Any time I see a cowboy in town, he gives us dark looks. I can feel the hatred out there. Not from town folks, but for anybody off a local ranch, and not just the Clantons'.'

'That McMasters boy rode in with a newcomer yesterday,' Louisa said. 'He tipped his hat and said, "Morning, Widow Earp".'

'I was with her, and heard it, too,' Virgil's Allie put in. 'It scared me, I don't mind admitting it.'

On the bed, Virgil grunted out a small laugh. 'That boy he was with is John Ringo. A known gunfighter. He joined up with the Clantons about a week ago. He's the kind of fellow Ike's hiring nowadays. He's bringing guns in. But it could be just for beefing up his raiding capability.'

'No,' Wyatt said quietly. 'It's for us.' Everybody in the room looked over at him. He was seated at a table with James, and volatile Morgan slumped on an easy chair near the bed.

'Well, they can't intimidate me!' Morgan growled.

'That's the point I'm making,' Mattie went on. 'You boys look at all this as just another challenge. But you're outgunned and outmanned, and the county sheriff is just sitting back and hoping the Clantons bury you! I hear that Ike has sworn he'll see all four of you in your coffins! I think it's time to step back and give all this some thought. What are we proving by staying on where we're not wanted? If Virgil wants to go on lawing with my Wyatt and Morgan, there are plenty of other towns in this territory that could benefit from our settling there.'

'We're the law here, Mattie,' Virgil told her. 'We're the only law here. What about these townsfolk who want a civilized place to live in, and not be terrorized by a bunch of lawless cowboys and gunmen? Who's going to uphold the law here if we don't? Johnny Behan?'

'We don't care who upholds the law here!' Louisa cried out. 'This is a problem for federal marshals, or the army! You're three against a hundred! It's not fair!'

'It's always this way for town marshals, Louisa,' James replied to her. 'Wyatt had the same thing in Dodge City. And when he left, the town was liveable for civilized folks. Anyway, we're invested here, girls. Wyatt and Virgil sank their money into the Oriental, and I got a good job there. We're settled in.'

'Exactly,' Morgan agreed.

'I think this will all quiet down one of these days soon,' Virgil offered. His thick legs were crossed on the bed, his feet boot-less. He was paring his nails with a small pruning knife. 'I don't think Ike sees us as a real threat to his illegal activities.'

Wyatt leaned forward on his chair. 'Well, Virgil, I'm not sure that's true,' he said in his well-modulated voice. He sounded more like an attorney than a sometime lawman.

Virgil cast a mildly surprised look toward him, and the room went silent. Wyatt was admitted to be the smartest of the brothers. He was also the best with other people when he spoke. His manner was one of authority, of supreme confidence in his own opinions. People tended to pay attention when he talked, and to evaluate what he said. Also, of the four brothers, he was by far the fastest and most deadly with a gun, and was absolutely fearless in a gunfight, as he had proved over and over again in Kansas.

'When I see the likes of John Ringo, and Pony Deal, and Indian Charlie being recruited by the Clantons, I have to believe it's for more than cattle rustling. They see us as standing between them and complete ownership of this county. They haven't had to deal with anything like that before, and they're planning to do something about it.'

The room was deathly silent for a long moment, then Mattie spoke up again. 'Well, I'm glad you see what we girls have been saying. We can't stay on here and wait for the Clantons to build an army against us, Wyatt.'

'You're right, we can't all stay,' Wyatt went on.

'Oh, thank God!' Attie reacted.

Wyatt turned to her. 'The women have to leave,' he added.

'What!' Mattie cried out.

Even the men were staring at him curiously. James shook his head. 'Now, wait a minute, Wyatt. Isn't that a little extreme?'

'I'd have to agree with James, Wyatt,' Virgil said. 'Life would be terrible here without our women.'

'What can you be thinking, brother?' Morgan said quizzically.

Wyatt looked over at him soberly. 'If we stay here, we're asking for trouble, and we all know it. We brothers can handle that trouble. Maybe. But we don't want to expose the women to it. How do you know some drunken cowboy won't lose his sense and fire on one of them? It will be too late after it happens. No, the women have to leave. I'm sending them back to California, to join Warren there.' Warren was the fifth brother, in business on the West Coast. 'When this thing is over, we can send for all of you again.'

'Well, I'm not leaving without you!' dark-haired, pretty Mattie exclaimed. She went over and threw her arms around Wyatt. 'We want to stay with our men! Don't we, girls?'

'Yes, we're staying!' Louisa yelled out.

'I'm not leaving Virgil!' Allie joined in.

Wyatt took Mattie'a arms off him, and set her down at an empty chair at the table. 'Listen to me. There's no other way. You have no vote in this, Mattie. I'm doing this for your own safety.'

'I suppose it is the best thing,' Virgil said, swinging his legs off the bed, and taking a deep breath in.

'I don't like it,' Morgan complained. 'Who's going to cook for me? I can't boil an egg, Wyatt!'

Mattie stood up angrily. 'Well, I'm not going! I'll move out and get my own room! Until you four come to your senses!'

Wyatt sighed. He and Virgil were in their shirtsleeves, but Morgan and James still wore their dark coats. 'I won't let you do that, Mattie. I'm sorry. I'll write you regular till we get together again.'

Tears welled up in Mattie's eyes. 'You don't love me, Wyatt Earp! You prefer your lawing over a domestic life,

27

you always have!' Then she turned and ran out of the room.

Louisa shook her head. 'I'll go after her,' she said.

She and Allie followed Mattie from the room, and then the men were alone there. They all sat around disconsolately.

'Are you sure about this?' Morgan said to Wyatt at last.

'I'm sure,' Wyatt told him.

By mid-afternoon of the next day, the women were gone.

The following week went very quietly. Sheriff Behan stopped in at Virgil's small office on Allen Street and gave him a friendly warning, though.

'I thought you might like to know, Virgil. There's a real gathering out at the Clantons' place. Pony Deal and John Ringo are just the tip of the iceberg. Curly Bill Brocius rode in the other day, and they also got people like Pete Spence and Hank Swilling that can shoot a gun. Things are heating up around here, and I don't want to see no more killings.'

'We're peace-loving men, Johnny,' Virgil told him. 'We won't be responsible for making any trouble. I suggest you go out and talk to Ike Clanton.'

'I've done that,' Behan said. 'But you know Ike. You can't talk to him.'

'Well, then we'll let the chips fall where they may,' Virgil told him tightly.

A couple of days later Virgil and Morgan were playing cards in the San Pedro gaming house when three of Clanton's men came in and sat at a table near them. They were three recent additions to the Clanton trail hands: Pony Deal, John Ringo, and Curly Bill Brocius. They ordered a deck of cards, and began casting furtive glances toward the Earp table.

'Do you notice a strange smell in here?' Deal said to his companions as Brocius dealt them a hand. Deal was a gunfighter turned cowboy, and was always ready for a fight. He wore a stubble of beard, and his vest was greasy-looking. He and his cohorts all wore trail-colored Stetsons.

Morgan looked over at their table with a frown, but beefy Virgil put a hand on his arm. 'Let it go,' he said quietly. He laid a chip down on the table, and studied his hand.

'Oh, say, I just noticed!' Deal went on. 'There's some Earps in here! You think maybe that's where the stink is coming from?'

Morgan turned again. 'You'll push that saucy line too far, Pony,' he said in a low growl.

Deal laughed at that, and the other two joined in. 'Did you hear something from over there!' Deal asked them. 'It was so quiet, I thought maybe a rat was squeaking under the table!'

More laughter, as Morgan fumed. Virgil sighed. 'It's your play, Morgan. Let's keep the game going.'

'I don't know,' Brocius was saying. He was a tall, brawny man with curly, reddish hair showing under his Stetson. He was known to be a cold-blooded killer, and had been a favorite of old man Clanton. 'It sounded more like a weasel to me. A dirty, nasty little weasel. But I could be wrong.'

'No, I think you're right,' John Ringo interjected. He had thick, dark hair and a pencil-thin mustache that made him look rather debonair. But he dressed in rawhides and Mexican boots, and had a tough, Latin look. He wore a yellow kerchief at his neck, and had a cultured manner that belied a wanton nature. He had met Doc Holliday in Kansas, and an enmity had grown between them. 'The stink is more like a weasel than a rat.'

Virgil looked over at them. 'Why don't you boys just play cards and mind your business over there?' he said a bit loudly.

Pony Deal turned to face him. 'Are you talking to us, Earp?'

'That's right,' Virgil said. 'We don't want any trouble with you. We're here to play cards. Now just let it go.'

'Are you telling us we can't talk in here?' Brocius spat out.

'Yeah. We don't like being told we can't talk,' Ringo spoke up again, grinning slightly. 'You got authority to stop talking in here, Earp?'

'I didn't say anything about not talking,' Virgil frowned. 'Now, just let us play cards.'

'You know,' Brocius said, 'I don't think I like sitting in this weasel stink. I think you and that other weasel ought to just get up and leave, Marshal.'

Morgan was red-faced. He turned hotly toward Brocius, and his hand went out over his gun. At the other table, all three men moved their gunhands free for use.

'You got something you want to say, weasel?' Ringo asked Morgan.

'Turn around, Morgan,' Virgil urged him.

'No, we want to find out what this stinking weasel has to say to us,' Pony Deal insisted.

Virgil scowled toward them, and Brocius scraped his chair away from their table, readying himself. But just at that moment, the swinging doors at the front of the room parted and Wyatt Earp walked in.

Brocius saw him first, and his whole body posture

changed. He poked Ringo, then all three men were watching Wyatt approach. Wyatt had sensed the tension between the tables as soon as he cleared the doors. Now he closed fluidly on the two tables, spurs clinking softly. He wore his black coat jacket and his stiff-brimmed black Stetson. The two Peacemaker Colts stuck out menacingly from under the open coat. Virgil saw his entrance, and nodded to Morgan, who smiled slightly. There were several other customers in the room, who had been listening to the exchange between the tables, and now all their eyes were on Wyatt.

Wyatt stopped between the two tables, and nodded to his brothers. 'Virgil. Morgan.'

'We've been waiting for you to join us, Wyatt,' Virgil said.

Wyatt turned to the other table. 'You looked like you were about to say something to my brothers here, Bill,' he said to Brocius. 'Don't let me interrupt.'

Brocius wiped a hand across his mouth, and pulled his chair back to the table. He swallowed hard. 'No, that's all over, Wyatt,' he said in a changed voice. 'We was all just having sport with each other. Ain't that right, Virgil?'

Virgil just glared at him. Wyatt turned to Ringo, who sat very subdued now. 'What about you, John? You want to make any comments about Virgil's card-playing? He's always open to suggestions.'

Ringo just looked up at him sourly. 'I wouldn't presume,' he said. 'I'm pretty lousy at cards myself.'

Wyatt turned to Pony Deal, another of the Clanton favorites. 'I notice you boys are carrying, Pony.'

Deal just looked up at him with a scowl. Everybody knew there was an ordinance against carrying sidearms in town, passed because of Virgil, but the Earps didn't enforce it unless the individual involved was causing trouble.

Deal responded at last. 'What's your point, Marshal?'

'Well, you know that's a violation, boys. I'm going to have to ask you to turn your guns over to the house manager, or get on your mounts and ride out.' He pushed his coat away from the two guns on his hips, and a heavy silence fell over the room.

Deal's face turned crimson, and his hand dropped down to his side. 'Ask all you want, Earp. We take our orders from Ike Clanton!'

Virgil and Morgan rose from their chairs, looking formidable, and Deal's face softened. His hand went back to the table. Ringo was eyeing the Colts on Wyatt's hips, and was remembering what Wyatt had done at the corral shoot-out. 'You can't do this, Wyatt. We're just playing a friendly game of cards here.'

Wyatt spoke to Virgil without taking his eyes off the other table. 'Is that the way you saw it, Marshal?'

'It was getting pretty stiff in here when you walked in,' Virgil said.

'Curly Bill had his juice up,' Morgan added darkly.

'Aw, I was just funning,' Brocius said, trying a hard grin.

Wyatt nodded. 'Well, you have your choice, boys. Just turn those guns over and you can go on with your game.' In a level, easy voice.

Pony Deal looked over at John Ringo and Brocius to see their reaction to Wyatt's demand. They all just sat there for a long moment, then Brocius slammed some cards onto the table angrily, and came off his chair like a cougar. 'You're going to live to regret this, Earp! Mark my words!' Then he stormed out of the place, with Pony Deal right behind him, hurling a blistering look at Virgil as he passed him.

John Ringo rose, too, deliberately adjusting the gunbelt on his hip. He gave Wyatt a cold, deadly look as he turned to follow the others. 'You better order up three coffins from Mr Ream, boys. It looks like you're going to need them.'

A moment later he was gone, too. Virgil and Morgan sat back down, and Wyatt joined them. 'Now,' he said casually, 'why don't you go ahead and deal the cards, Morgan? I'd like to squeeze a nice game in before supper.'

The Clanton gunhands stayed out of Tombstone for a while after that confrontation, although Ike Clanton and his brother Phineas, or Phin, kept a room at the Grand Hotel, not far from the Cosmopolitan, where the Earps had their rooms, and they were in and out of there occasionally. The Earps never walked the streets alone now, even though the Clanton people made themselves scarce. Townsfolk were staying away from the Oriental saloon where James Earp worked and Wyatt had his money invested, because it was off limits to cowhands, and town people were afraid to offend the ranchers by patronizing the establishment. One morning the manager of the Oriental found a handwritten sign on the outside wall of the saloon, beside the front door. It read: CLOSED DUE TO INCLEMENT CLIMATE.

The sign was torn down by mid-morning, but a lot of locals had seen it, and saw it as a warning to keep away.

That afternoon Doc Holliday joined Wyatt and James at the saloon. James was so disgruntled about business that he threatened to quit his job there and go across the street to the Eagle Brewery. Wyatt and James were drinking black coffee, but Doc ordered whiskey for medicinal purposes.

'You better let the boss buy you out while your interest

is still worth something,' James was saying to Wyatt. 'The ranchers are going to put us out of business. We have no way to fight back.'

Sallow-faced Doc swigged his drink. 'We can call them out again. Make the corral look like a Sunday picnic. Gun down all the Clanton mercenaries in one big play. Then we'd have this town back. People won't even come to me to have a tooth pulled. They're like scared rabbits.'

Wyatt smiled a half-smile. 'There's too many now, Doc. Call them all together and you face an army. If we're patient, though, they'll get in trouble one at a time. We have badges, and they don't. That may not seem like an advantage, but it is. For instance, Virgil has word that Pete Spence might have held up that stage a couple weeks ago. And maybe he had another Clanton hand with him.'

'Spence?' James said incredulously. 'I didn't think he was that dumb. I can't believe Ike would approve something like that.'

Wyatt shrugged. 'We don't have enough evidence yet to make arrests. Maybe we never will. But that's the kind of thing I'm talking about. If we're patient, these people will make mistakes. And we'll be there.'

James shook his head. 'You and Virgil seem to thrive on this, Wyatt. But I don't. What I should be doing is just pulling up stakes. This isn't my kind of game.'

'It's exactly my kind.' Doc grinned. His side wound was healing badly, but he paid little attention to it. 'I'd especially like to face down John Ringo. That boy's been slandering me behind my back ever since Kansas.'

'Ringo's easy manner hides the heart of a cold-blooded killer,' Wyatt observed. 'He's dangerous, Doc. So is Brocius. Don't let them gang up on you.'

'I'll shoot it out with all of them if they want it,' Doc

responded darkly. He coughed heavily into a handkerchief, and the other two watched him somberly.

'How have you been feeling, Doc?' James asked him.

Doc looked over at him with a frown. 'Just fine,' he growled. 'Why do you ask?'

James colored a little. 'Why, no special reason, Doc. I'm just interested in the welfare of a friend.'

'You didn't ask Wyatt how he felt,' Doc commented caustically. 'How come you're always asking me?'

'It's a legitimate question, Doc,' Wyatt intervened smoothly. 'No offense was meant.'

Doc rubbed a hand across his mouth, and swigged the rest of his drink. 'Don't mind me. It's just that it's in the back of my head all the time. It's going to jump up and bite me in the hindquarters one of these days, and I won't be able to shoot my way out of it. So there it is. I try to act like it's not happening. Sorry, James.'

'No offense taken, Doc,' James assured him.

Wyatt changed the subject. 'The Clantons are capable of almost anything. That means we all have to watch our backs. I suggested to Virgil that we partner up on night patrols, but he doesn't stick to that. Thinks it makes us look scared.'

Doc grinned. 'I don't think anybody in his right mind would accuse you of that, Wyatt,' he suggested. 'At least, nobody who knows you from Kansas.'

'Well, he goes out regular by himself,' Wyatt said. 'I can't stop him. But sometimes I keep an eye on him from the Oriental. Morgan has been so involved in riding stage for Wells, Fargo that he doesn't do much marshaling, and maybe that's not so bad.' He looked over at the bar, where two patrons had just walked in. They were townsfolk, not cowboys. 'Looks like you're going to have to attend to some business, James. I think I'll just take a stroll down Allen Street to look things over. Care to accompany me, Doc?'

Doc nodded. 'I need the exercise. You take good care of those customers, James. You're going to need their patronage.'

James grinned. 'Maybe even more than you suppose, Doc.'

'And I apologize for my rude behavior,' Doc added. 'I'm a well-known social misfit, you know. I'll behave better next time.'

'No need, Doc,' James assured him. 'Our affection for you is as firm as bedrock.'

They had all risen. Wyatt threw some coins onto the table, and smiled. 'Don't make the man embarrassed, James. He's not accustomed to compliments.'

Doc gave him a mock frown, and the two of them left the place.

A few days later, in mid-evening, Virgil and Wyatt were playing cards on a pickle barrel at the Union Market, a general store, and beefy Virgil was getting one bad hand after another. Eventually he threw his cards down and rose from his chair.

'Did you mark these cards for my brother?' he called peevishly to the storekeeper who stood behind a long counter.

'Them cards is brand-new, Marshal!' the heavy-set fellow called back. 'You just never learned how to use them!'

'Sit down, Virgil,' Wyatt told him. 'I'll go get a pinochle deck.'

'No, I'm kind of restless tonight,' Virgil said. 'I'm going

down the street to see how things are at the Oriental.'

'I'll walk with you.'

Virgil frowned at him. 'I don't need no minder, Wyatt. We been through this. You got to buy some coffee for Morgan before you leave. I'll see you at the Oriental.'

Wyatt sighed. 'All right, big brother. Keep your pants on. I'll catch up with you shortly. Just watch yourself out there.'

Virgil gave him a sour look and left. Wyatt got up and went over to the storekeeper. 'Make that two pounds of the Colombian,' he said. 'Morgan won't drink any other kind.'

Outside on the street several shots were fired, reverberating in the night.

'Good heavens!' the clerk exclaimed. 'What was that?'

But Wyatt was already on his way out, his Colt quickly drawn. When he got out on the street, he immediately saw Virgil, sprawled on the ground, gun in hand, looking into the darkness. Wyatt scanned the street and saw nothing. He ran over to his brother, and knelt over him.

Virgil was holding his side and blood was seeping through his shirt.

'They only hit me once,' he gasped out. 'It's buckshot. I think I'm all right.'

Wyatt holstered his gun, and examined the wound. 'It's not bad. Who was it, Virgil?'

'It's awful dark out here. But I think I saw Ike Clanton. There were three of them, Wyatt.' Gritting it out.

Wyatt looked up, and swore under his breath. The boldness of it was incredible: to ambush and gun down a town marshal right on Allen Street. Very few had taken their threats seriously, but Wyatt had. Now they had shown their true colors. As he had suspected, they were dealing with back-shooters. And their aim was to take all the Earps out. Or scare them back to Kansas.

'Do you think you can stand?' Wyatt asked him. 'I can get you to the doctor. He's right down the street.'

Virgil nodded. Wyatt helped him up and Virgil threw an arm over Wyatt's shoulder. 'I might have hit one of them,' he said.

Just then an old man came out onto the street and spoke to them. 'I heard you talking. It was Ike, all right. And brother Phin. I think the third one was Pony Deal.'

'Will you swear to that?' Wyatt asked him.

'Oh, no!' the old fellow responded. 'That would be my death warrant!'

'He's old man Grimshaw,' Virgil gasped. He had been hit with a shotgun blast from the rear, and his arm was bleeding as well as his side.

'We'll be talking to you later,' Wyatt said. Then he and Virgil headed off toward the doctor's house, just a short distance away, Virgil leaning heavily on Wyatt.

It seemed the blood vendetta that Wyatt anticipated had begun.

CHAPTER THREE

Virgil's wounds weren't fatal ones, but they required some healing time. While Virgil rested the burden fell on Wyatt and Morgan to keep the peace, and to find evidence to arrest the Clanton brothers and their hired gun. Old man Grimshaw withdrew his statement about having seen the Clantons, and insisted he hadn't been able to see clearly enough to identify anyone. Wyatt went to Sheriff Behan to gain his support in arresting Ike Clanton, based only on Virgil's statement, but Behan rightly insisted that that wasn't enough for an arrest.

'Well, you tell your crony Ike that justice will be served, one way or the other,' Wyatt warned Behan. 'Virgil is lucky he isn't dead. If you don't stand behind us, John, you're going to have a real war right here in Tombstone. And the Earps are up for a war, if that's what you want.'

'Nobody wants a war, Wyatt,' Behan assured him. 'If you can get Grimshaw to make a statement, maybe we'll have something. But the way things stand now, we'd never get a conviction against anybody.'

Wyatt stood nose to nose with him. 'This was my brother, John. My brother. I know you're no killer. But if you stand with killers, that could be a dangerous piece of ground to be on. If you understand me.'

Behan met his steely look. 'I'm neutral in this, Wyatt. You won't get any trouble from me.'

'I hope you remember that,' Wyatt told him.

Back at the Cosmopolitan Hotel that afternoon Wyatt found his brothers and Doc Holliday sitting around in Wyatt's quarters commiserating with Virgil. Virgil was reclining in a big, overstuffed chair, with a shirt unbuttoned down the front, revealing a wide, thick bandage across his meaty ribs. The group was situated in the small parlor, and Morgan and James were seated on the sofa, looking glum. Doc was leaning against a wall facing the sofa. They all looked toward Wyatt as he entered the room.

'We wondered where you were,' Morgan said.

'Boys,' Wyatt greeted them. 'I just been talking to Behan. How are you feeling, Virgil?'

Virgil made a face. 'I been hurt worse than this falling off my mount. What did Behan have to say?'

'He says he's neutral,' Wyatt said flatly, easing himself into the other soft chair.

'That's a lie,' Doc offered from the wall. As he stood there, thin as a rail, the thing you saw first when you looked at him was the pair of Colt Peacemakers hanging boldly on his hips. 'Say the word and I'll quietly put that liar underground.'

Virgil gave him a sour look. 'I'm a peace officer, Doc. I don't operate that way. Neither does Wyatt.'

Doc shrugged. 'Mark my word. You'll have trouble from him before this is over.'

'I say we ride out to the Clanton ranch and make some arrests,' the hot-head Morgan said angrily. 'Before they shoot us all in the back, while Behan sits on his hands.'

'The county won't prosecute without hard evidence,' Wyatt said quietly from his chair. All eyes turned on him. He had removed his black Stetson and was running a hand through his dark hair. 'I don't blame old man Grimshaw, though. If the Clantons heard that he would testify against them, they'd kill him, for sure. He'd never get to trial.'

A stony silence fell into the room. 'Then what do we do?' Morgan said a little loudly. 'Just wait for them to kill one of us? Or throw our badges down and ride out? I like this town. James here is doing well with the Sampling Room saloon.'

'I'd rather give up my job than start a war with an army of cowpokes,' James offered softly.

'Morgan has a point, Wyatt,' Doc intervened. 'The Clantons are holding all the cards. They have numbers, and they're not bound by the law. Those badges you're wearing give them a big advantage. They can back-shoot you and Behan will look the other way. But you have to play by the rules. You're lawmen. Here's my idea. Take the badges off, go out there and shoot a few of them, and then go back to playing marshal again.'

'We're not playing at marshaling, Doc,' Virgil said evenly. 'We have roots here now. We want Tombstone to be a place where we can live. Live in peace.'

'There won't be any peace here till Ike Clanton is six feet under,' Doc said. 'And that might be impossible, working within the law.'

'I should have been with Virgil when he was shot,' Wyatt put in, not really listening to the conversation. He stared across the room. Deep in his own thoughts. 'I let Virgil talk me out of it. That won't happen again.'

'If you had been there you might be dead,' Virgil told him.

'If I had been there Ike Clanton might be dead,' Wyatt said.

Again, all present stared at him for a long moment, knowing that what he said was true.

'From now on, no exceptions,' Wyatt went on, looking over at Virgil. 'None of us goes out on the street alone.'

Virgil sighed. 'All right, Wyatt.'

'That goes for you, too, Doc,' Wyatt added, turning to his old friend.

'Hey, now wait a minute here. I'm not wearing a badge, and I don't take orders from anybody who does.'

'You're one of us, Doc,' James blurted out. 'Badge or not.'

'Doc,' Wyatt said softly. 'I'm asking you as a favor. Will you humor me in this?'

Doc blew his thin cheeks out, and stared at the floor for a moment. Then his gaze fell on Wyatt. 'Well. If you put it that way.'

Wyatt grinned a handsome grin, and rose from his chair. 'It's about time for James's turn at the Oriental. I'm walking him down there, and then stopping in at Bob Hatch's poolroom. Anybody up to a walk?'

'I'll go along,' Morgan said. 'I need some air.'

Doc Holliday pushed his lean frame off the wall. 'Me too. I owe Bob a double-eagle for some games.'

'Don't leave the place,' Wyatt told his older brother and town marshal Virgil. 'I'll bring you some antelope stew from the kitchen downstairs. I want you to rest.'

'Yes, Daddy,' Virgil replied with an acid look.

The streets were quiet that afternoon. They dropped James off at the Oriental saloon, where he would relieve Ned Boyle until the evening hours, when they would work the place together. Then Wyatt, Morgan and Doc walked on down to the pool hall. There were several mounts outside, picketed to the hitching rail, and Wyatt thought one of them belonged to Ike Clanton. When they got inside, his suspicions were confirmed.

There were just a half-dozen patrons present in the place. Two young locals were playing English billiards at a back table, and Ike Clanton was at a nearer one. With him were Billy Miller, John Ringo, and Hank Swilling. They were playing eight-ball pool. As soon as the threesome walked in they spotted the four players. Ike Clanton looked up and saw the newcomers, too.

Ike nudged Ringo, who stood next to him. 'Look at this.'

Wyatt and his companions stopped just inside the door. Doc looked over at Wyatt. 'Maybe we don't have to ride out to the ranch.' He grinned.

Wyatt met his gaze. 'You go settle your account with Bob, Doc.'

Doc frowned for a moment, but then his long, lean face relaxed. 'Sure, Marshal. Anything you say.'

The proprietor Bob Hatch had looked nervous from the moment they walked in. 'Well, hello, Doc. Boys. Can I offer you a table?'

'Just checking things out, Bob,' Wyatt answered. 'Doc wants to pay a bill.'

While Doc and Bob Hatch did business, Wyatt led Morgan over to the table where the Clanton people were playing. They both leaned against a wall that ran close to the table. Ike didn't look up at them again, but the other three stared tensely at Wyatt. Neither Wyatt nor Morgan said anything.

Ringo took his turn at the table. He knocked a ball into

a corner pocket, then missed on his next shot.

'Your shot, Hank,' Ike said to Swilling.

Swilling gave Wyatt and Morgan a hard look, then leaned over the table.

'How have you been, Ike?' Wyatt said suddenly.

Ike looked over at Wyatt. 'What's it to you, Marshal?'

Swilling rose from the table, not taking the shot. Ringo and Miller were staring morosely at Wyatt.

'Been in town at night lately?' Wyatt went on.

Ike laid his pool cue down. 'If I had, would that be a crime here in Tombstone?'

'I was just wondering if you were planning any more back-shoots,' Wyatt said with a half-smile. But his eyes weren't smiling. 'It's only fair to give your next victim a little notice, don't you think? Since you always come up from behind him.'

Ike's face went dark. 'You trying to say something, Earp?'

'Look, we all know you tried to kill my brother, Ike. But you didn't have the guts to face him down, did you? And you had to have help. You came at him like a pack of jackals.'

'You don't know what you're talking about, Earp. Now, why don't you go bother somebody else for a while? We got a game to play here.'

'You better shut up and pay attention, Ike!' Morgan said loudly.

Doc looked up from the counter where he was talking with Hatch.

'Do you understand the situation you'd have made for yourself if you'd killed my brother?' Wyatt said in a low, level voice.

Fear sprang into Hank Swilling's chest and caused him

44

to swallow hard. He also laid down his cue and stepped quietly away from the table. Ringo laid his gunhand on his gunbelt as Ike Clanton leaned on the table.

'Are you still here?' he said in an off-hand manner to Wyatt.

'I'll be moving on shortly,' Wyatt said. 'But I thought I'd take this opportunity to make you a little deal.'

'You? Make a deal?'

Doc, Bob Hatch, and the two other patrons were all listening to the banter now, too. Swilling was barely breathing. Billy Miller, a lean cowboy, watched with narrowed eyes. John Ringo's hand was still hanging on his belt.

'That's right,' Wyatt said. 'Since you and your paid guns are such bad shots, you barely wounded Virgil. You lost brother Billy at the corral, so Virgil is willing to call it a draw.'

Morgan looked over at Wyatt fiercely.

'In other words, we'll call a temporary truce if you're of a mind, so we can get some law enforcement done here in town.'

Ike stared at Wyatt for a long moment, trying to assess what was behind his eyes. 'Well, well. The law wants a truce.'

'It might also save some bloodshed,' Wyatt added. 'We all have to live here together, Ike. It might be a bit more pleasant if we weren't all shooting at each other all the time.'

Doc shook his head. 'Well, listen to that,' he said under his breath.

Morgan turned to Wyatt again. 'Wyatt. Virgil didn't—'

'Not now, Morgan,' Wyatt said easily.

Ike was grinning now. 'Now let me see if I've got this

straight. Because some unknown person or persons, none of whom were me or any of my people, shot the marshal the other night, you want a truce with me, who had nothing to do with it?'

'If you want to put it that way,' Wyatt told him.

'Hmm. Well, I say, Earp, that it's still one to nothing. Your favor. Not that that means you'll have any trouble from us, of course. But, listen. I hope you find the people who shot your brother. Now, can we go back to our pool game?'

'So you reject my offer?' Wyatt said soberly.

'There's no need for any truce, Earp. All you have to do is this. You and your brothers turn your badges in and ride back to Kansas, where they don't mind putting up with a family of gunslingers like you boys. Then things will get back to normal around here.'

'That's right,' Ringo added. 'Back to normal.'

Wyatt gave Ringo a sour look. 'You're a hired gun, John. How would you know what's normal around here?'

Ringo grinned crookedly.

'If things go back to normal,' Wyatt continued, 'this county will be terrorized by rustling, armed robbery and murder. Maybe you'd like that, Ike. But the citizens of Tombstone won't. If we leave, there won't be any law here.'

'Johnny Behan can enforce the law,' Ike said arrogantly. 'He don't need help from gunslingers.'

'John Behan does what you tell him,' Wyatt countered. 'And you can pass this on to him.' He pushed off the wall, and Morgan did, too. 'The Earps are staying. And they will enforce the law here.'

'I'm sure he'll want to hear that,' Ike replied. 'Now, I'm going to play me a game of pool, Marshal. Be sure to keep those night streets quiet for us.' A quiet laugh under his breath.

'You can count on it,' Wyatt said as he turned and walked over to where Doc was standing, Morgan following him closely.

'Why did you do that?' Doc said when he arrived there.

'Somebody had to try to stop the insanity,' Wyatt replied gravely. 'I didn't think he'd respond to reason. But I had to try.'

'He'll just take it as a sign of weakness on our part,' Morgan complained.

'Then that gives us an advantage, doesn't it?' Wyatt said.

'The citizens of Tombstone will appreciate it,' Bob Hatch said.

Wyatt glanced at him. 'Thanks, Bob. Well, come on, Morgan. We'll make our afternoon rounds. We still have our jobs to do. What about you, Doc?'

'We could have done it right here,' Doc said bitterly. 'All four of them. And it would be over. It would only leave Phin, and he doesn't have the guts for it.'

'He has Brocius, Indian Charlie and a lot of others to do his fighting for him,' Wyatt reminded him. 'Anyway, Ike would never draw down on me. I doubt that even Ringo would.'

'Then you make it happen, anyway,' Doc said. 'When you find a snake, you step on it. You don't reason with it.'

Wyatt let out long breath. 'Let's go, Morgan. Are you staying, Doc?'

'I'm just going to palaver with Bob a while.'

'Stay away from them,' Wyatt warned him. 'I mean it, Doc.'

'Has anybody told you you're getting a little bossy?' Doc said.

A moment later, Wyatt and Morgan were gone.

A couple of weeks passed quietly then, after Wyatt's confrontation with Ike Clanton. Ike and his brother Phineas would spend an occasional night at the Grand Hotel after a late evening at the saloons or poolroom. They kept a suite of rooms there for themselves and some of their top hands. But they were not causing any trouble now, and Wyatt began to wonder whether Ike had, after all, accepted his peace treaty. Virgil had no problem with Wyatt's offering a truce, and told the others that he would have done the same thing when he saw Ike again. He had healed now, and was back out on the street, usually with Wyatt and sometimes with Morgan, making a show of strength. Morgan got over his irritatiion with Wyatt, and concluded, as the days passed, that Wyatt had scared Ike away from making any further trouble.

At the Clanton ranch, things weren't quiet at all. Men like John Ringo, Curly Bill Brocius and Pete Spence were telling Ike Clanton that they would have trouble with the Earps as long as they were in Tombstone, and that despite their failure with Virgil, it should be easy to take them all down if they planned it all carefully.

As for Virgil, his arm was still weeping from the gunshot wound, and he wasn't healing as well as they had previously thought. After a few days back on the job he was feeling the pain quite a bit, and Wyatt insisted he get some more bed rest until the wound healed properly.

'I don't need a damn nursemaid, Wyatt!' Virgil yelled at his brother. 'This will heal up if you just quit watching over it! I'm needed down at the office!'

But in the end, Wyatt prevailed. Virgil agreed to see the

doctor again, and the doctor removed some more buckshot from Virgil shoulder, and recommended a week of rest.

Wyatt and Morgan manned the town marshal's office, and did the street patrols for a while then. They saw Ike Clanton in town a couple of times, usually with Pony Deal or John Ringo, but Ike never spoke to them. Ringo always seemed to have a grin on his Latin face, and once he even tipped his hat to them. On another occasion, Doc Holliday was out on the street with Morgan, and as soon as Doc and Ringo saw each other, their faces went straight-lined. There was a long-standing enmity between them that Doc never talked about.

One cool evening Wyatt and Morgan walked down to Hatch's Poolroom again, because restless Morgan wanted to shoot some games. He was slightly depressed about Virgil's slow recovery, and in no mood for paperwork at the office, or posting Wanted dodgers on a bulletin board. When they arrived there were several customers busily engaged in games at two separate tables. A table was open at the rear of the place, near a back door, and Bob Hatch set them up there. Two ranch hands from Ike Clanton's ranch had been playing at one of the tables when the Earps entered. After a brief time they cast hard looks at the Earps, then left.

'Don't mind them, Wyatt,' Hatch said when they were gone. 'They only know what they're told out there.'

'Most of them wouldn't be bad boys if they worked somewhere else,' Wyatt commented.

'They don't work somewhere else,' Morgan observed acidly, as he set out the pool balls. 'They work for the Clantons, and they're Clanton men.'

Wyatt took off his black coat, and Morgan followed suit.

Then Wyatt broke to start the game, and two balls went down.

'Here we go again,' Morgan complained. 'I never get a chance when I play with you, brother! You're as good with that cue stick as you are with those Peacemakers. I don't know why I bother.'

'It's pretty much luck on the break,' Wyatt said. 'You'll catch up.'

He took a second shot and knocked the six ball into a corner pocket. Morgan sighed. Without his coat on he looked quite slim. Wyatt was the brother who was well-muscled, and looked rather athletic. Beefy Virgil carried too much weight. Wyatt shot a third time and narrowly missed dumping another ball into a side pocket. Across the room, the only other players in the hall paid up and also left.

Wyatt watched the last patrons leave. They looked like townsfolk. He turned back to Morgan. 'OK, brother. The table is all yours. Take them down.'

Morgan leaned into make a shot, when the swinging slatted doors at the front pushed open and Virgil entered, with Doc Holliday.

'I told you they'd be here,' Doc said to Virgil, who was wearing a sling on his left arm.

'Hey, Virgil's here!' Morgan said loudly. 'And Doc.'

'Come on in, boys,' Bob Hatch cried out from behind his counter. 'Your friends over there drove my other paying customers out of here!' A slow grin played across his features.

'Bob.' Doc greeted him. He walked on past the proprietor and over to the Earps' table. 'Are you winning yet, Morgan?'

'You know Wyatt. He hardly ever misses,' Morgan

groused. 'I haven't hardly had a chance to play yet.'

Wyatt handed Doc his cue stick. 'Here. See if you can quiet him down to a yell. I'll be back shortly.'

Doc took the stick. 'Well, Morgan. Looks like you finally found a player you can beat.'

As Morgan leaned over the table again for his first shot, Wyatt walked over to where Virgil was leaning on the counter, talking with Hatch. Wyatt leaned beside him.

'Are you sure you're up to this night stuff? You told me you were spending the evening reading the *Epitaph*.'

'I got tired of that,' Virgil said flatly. 'Do I have to check with you to go out now?'

'You promised me you wouldn't go out at night without one of us,' Wyatt said.

'Doc came past. He's one of us.'

'You're not letting that wound heal,' Wyatt said.

'Wyatt. Please, just quit talking about it,' big Virgil responded. 'By the way. When we came past the Oriental, Ike Clanton was just going in. He had his favorite foremen with him. Pete Spence, John Ringo, Curly Bill, and Pony Deal. The thing that surprised me was seeing Frank Stilwell with them.'

'Stilwell? Behan's deputy? Are you sure?' Wyatt wondered.

'I'm sure. Doc saw him, too.'

'I probably shouldn't be saying this,' Hatch put in. 'But there's talk that Frank was with a couple of Clanton boys at that stage hold-up last month.'

'We know,' Wyatt said.

'He's also been seen out at the Clanton ranch a couple times,' Hatch went on. 'Maybe I should have told you boys.'

'He's a weak sister with big ambitions,' Virgil

commented. 'He probably figures he can't wait out Behan to wear the sheriff's badge himself.'

'I can't imagine why Ike would even be interested in him,' Wyatt observed. 'Unless he thinks he can use Stilwell for some advantage. Maybe Stilwell promised him some special service.'

'I wouldn't trust him for a special job,' Virgil commented.

'Well, I got some tabs to add up, gentlemen,' Hatch said. He headed down the counter toward the rear of the place, and suddenly stopped in his tracks. 'Hey. Is that somebody trying to get in through the back door?'

Wyatt and Virgil both turned and saw shadowy figures through the glass in the rear door. Wyatt caught the dim flash of metal, and his face changed.

'Morgan! Doc! Get down!'

But in the next instant, as Wyatt drew a Peacemaker, two loud blasts came through the rear door, shattering glass and making a reverberating din in the quiet of the pool hall. Morgan's back was to the door, as he leaned over the pool table to take another shot. He had sunk two balls and was feeling good. Almost simultaneous with the shots he felt the clubbing in his back, one of the shots hitting him directly in the spine. A third shot came, and went wild. Wyatt and Doc both returned fire, but the men behind the glass were already gone.

'Morgan!' Virgil yelled out.

'Oh, no!' Hatch muttered. 'Oh, God, no!'

'Doc, take care of Morgan!' Wyatt yelled. Then he was running to the rear door, kicking it open, and pushing through it into the night.

Outside, there was no sign of the shooters. He ran down the back street and looked around again. Then, out on Allen Street, there was the sound of horses galloping away. When he got out there, they were gone.

He saw a scared-looking boy standing under the canopy of a building, and went over to him.

'Did you see those men?' he asked the boy.

The boy hesitated. 'Yes, Marshal.'

'Who were they, boy? It's important.'

The young man hesitated again. 'One was Mr Stilwell.'

'Mr Stilwell? Are you sure?'

'I think so.'

'And there was another man?'

'Yes, sir. Two of them. One was that fellow Pete Spence. I seen him in the Union Market a couple of times. Buying stuff for Ike Clanton.'

Wyatt swore under his breath. 'And the third?'

'It was some Indian. I never seen him before.'

Indian Charlie, Wyatt said to himself.

'I hope that helps, Marshal.'

'You did real well, boy. Thanks.'

A moment later Wyatt was back inside, hurrying to Morgan's side. Hatch and Doc had laid Morgan on the pool table, on his back, and he looked bad. Virgil was leaning over him, his eyes tearing up.

'Oh, Morgan!'

'How bad is it?' Wyatt asked, breathless.

Doc looked over at him. 'He was hit twice. Once in the spine.'

'I can't feel my legs,' Morgan said weakly from the table. 'Why can't I feel my legs, Wyatt?'

'Just lay quiet, brother,' Wyatt told him. 'You're going to be all right. Bob went for the doctor. He'll fix you right up.'

Morgan coughed up some blood, and grinned. 'I

reckon playing pool can be downright dangerous.' In a very weak voice: 'Maybe I'll have to give it up.'

'Don't talk, Morgan,' Virgil implored him, his voice cracking.

'Maybe he needs a swig of whiskey,' Doc suggested.

'I'm not sure . . . I can wait for the doctor,' Morgan gasped out, as Doc wiped crimson from his cheek. 'Wyatt.'

'Yes, Morgan.'

'You get those . . . dirty bushwhackers. Will you?'

'We'll do that, Morgan. Now, just rest.'

'I'm real glad . . . come out here,' Morgan said in a rattling whisper. 'I don't regret. . . .'

There was another ragged coughing, and Morgan's eyes closed. A shudder passed through him, and he was lifeless. Doc touched a place on his throat, feeling for a pulse. Then he looked up at the brothers and shook his head.

'No,' Virgil muttered. 'No.'

At that moment Bob Hatch returned. James Earp was with him. Young James came and looked down at Morgan, his face white.

'He didn't make it,' Wyatt told him.

James gasped, clapping a hand over his mouth.

'I guess we won't need that doctor after all,' Hatch said somberly. 'I asked around out there, Wyatt. Nobody saw anything.'

When Wyatt turned to Hatch, his face was dangerous-looking. 'I found a witness,' he said. 'I know who those dirty cowards are, all right. But I can't use the witness. He's just a kid.'

'Who was it?' Virgil said loudly. 'Let's make some arrests before the trail gets cold!'

'Arrests?' Wyatt said in a different, cold voice. 'I don't think so.'

Virgil walked over to him. 'What do you mean, Wyatt? We have to do something!'

Wyatt sighed. 'Even if we used the kid, they'd find a way to avoid prosecution. I've lost confidence in the justice system here, Virgil. Doc was right. You can't fight people like this wearing badges.' He removed the deputy marshal's badge from his coat, which he had just put back on. He placed the badge on the counter, and then stared at Virgil. Virgil hesitated a moment, and then removed his own badge and laid it beside Wyatt's.

Wyatt turned to Bob Hatch. 'You know Mayor Clum pretty well, don't you, Bob?'

Hatch nodded. 'Sure, Wyatt.'

'You deliver these badges to him. You can get Morgan's off his coat over there. Tell him that this is no longer the law against the Clantons. It's the Earps.'

Hatch nodded. 'I'll tell him, Wyatt.' Swallowing hard.

'Yes, you tell him!' an angry James yelled out.

'And if the mayor sees Ike Clanton,' Wyatt began.

But then the front doors swung again, and Ike walked in with Ringo and Pony Deal. A deadly silence filled the room, and the only sound was the clinking of their spurs as they moved in and stopped near Wyatt and Virgil. Neither brother said a word.

'I hoped we'd find you here,' Ike spoke up. 'We heard about Morgan, Wyatt. Is he all right?'

'You damn vultures!' James blurted out.

'He's dead,' Wyatt answered smoothly. His urge was to draw on Clanton right there. But he had two fast guns with him, and neither James nor Virgil would be any good in a draw-down, and he might get them killed.

Ike put on a look of concern. 'Why, that's real bad, boys. Real bad luck. Of course, you have our condolences.

We all thought Morgan was a real fine lawman. Was it a shoot-out?'

'It was a back-shooting,' Wyatt said in a grating voice. 'Just like with Virgil.'

Ike frowned. 'Well, what do you say? I guess it ain't safe to play pool any more. Did you find out who did such a thing?'

'You know who did it!' Virgil said loudly.

John Ringo grinned slightly.

'Yes. I know who did it,' Wyatt said clearly and firmly.

Ike's face sagged slightly, and Ringo and Deal exchanged a look.

'Well, I hope it's nobody I know,' Ike finally managed.

'You know them,' Wyatt replied. 'And they will be brought to justice.'

Bob Hatch was holding his breath through all this, trying not to breathe. He expected an explosive gunfight to break out at any moment. Over at the table holding Morgan, Doc stepped quietly away from it with his hands on the grips of his Peacemakers.

'I hope you have better luck than you did when Virgil was shot,' Ike said evenly, getting his composure back.

'Oh, this will be different,' Wyatt said. 'This time we won't be depending on the local law.'

Ike glanced over to the counter. For the first time he saw the badges lying there and a small prickle of fear ran down his back. 'What's that? You boys resigned your posts?'

'That's right,' Wyatt said in a low, hard voice. 'Now we won't be hogtied with niceties, Ike. We'll be free to follow our own consciences without restraint.'

'That sounds dangerous, Earp,' Pony Deal said in a threatening voice.

'Yes,' John Ringo said. His yellow neckerchief gave an elegant look to his neat rawhides and belied his cold nature. 'Very dangerous.'

'Oh, I think these boys will use common sense in this,' Ike suggested. 'They won't kill a man without evidence of his guilt, I'm sure.'

'You tell the men involved in this,' Wyatt growled out. 'They're walking dead men. They might as well pick out their spots at Boot Hill.'

Ike arched his brow and stuck out his lantern jaw. 'I can't imagine how you think I'd know these men. But I wish you luck in any new endeavors you take on. I guess you boys will be moving on, then?'

'We won't be burying Morgan here in this sewer of the West,' Wyatt told him. 'I'm taking him out of here, and sending him home. If anybody harasses us on the way out, I warn you, Ike, I'll take a half-dozen of them down.'

Ike shook his head. 'That would be sacrilege, Wyatt. You have our blessing. Go in peace.' He hesitated. 'But a little free advice. Don't come back.'

With that, Ike turned and left again, with Ringo giving Wyatt a pleasant grin as they walked out.

CHAPTER FOUR

Over the next couple of days, while the town undertakers Ritter and Ream built a double-strong coffin for Morgan to travel in, James quit his job at the Oriental saloon and Wyatt sold his interest in the establishment to his partner Lou Rickabaugh. Virgil, who was fairly well healed from his wounds but still feeling some pain in his arm, had a visit from Mayor Clum, who attempted to persuade Virgil and his brothers to stay on 'until things cool off'. But Virgil and Wyatt both realized now that to remain in Tombstone would be extremely dangerous under these conditions. It was clear now that Ike Clanton intended to use his entire small army of ranch hands to seek out, ambush and murder all the brothers if they stayed on.

'This is warfare, boys,' Wyatt told his brothers as they stood over Morgan in his coffin on that cool day in early 1882, preparing to leave town the following day. 'And we're up against a battalion of armed bushwhackers. If we stay here now, we die. Once we get Morgan safely gone, we have to start waging this war on our terms. We have to pick the time and place for our battles. The terrain, the conditions. We may not be able to defeat their army. But we can make the men who murdered Morgan pay.'

Doc Holliday was there, too. 'I'm glad to hear you say that, Wyatt. You can count me to be there with you.'

'I appreciate that, Doc.'

James and Virgil stood with their hats in hand, staring down at the death face of Morgan. 'They wanted a feud,' Virgil said thickly. 'Well, now they've got one.'

James was shaking his head. 'What surprises me is that Frank Stilwell would be dumb enough to involve himself in this. I mean, the deputy sheriff?'

'Stilwell is a brash young hot-head who has his own ideas about getting along in the world,' Wyatt said. 'I doubt very much that Behan knows that he was in on it. Stilwell probably figures Ike owes him now. He might want Behan's job.'

'That kid has earned himself six feet of ground in a quiet place,' Doc growled. Doc had liked Morgan for his fiery temper, and his fierce loyalty to his brothers.

Wyatt turned to James. 'You get down here early tomorrow, to get the box loaded onto the wagon. It's all arranged with the undertaker. Doc will be with you. Virgil and I will pack up some things and meet you here at eight.'

James nodded. 'We'll be ready to go when you get here.'

'We'll ride to Contention where the California train comes through, and put Morgan on there. You can accompany the body. When you get to California, tell Warren to stay put. He's no more a gunman than you are.'

Wyatt turned and left the funeral parlor; the others followed him. Out on the street, though, James confronted Wyatt. 'I'm not going to California.'

'What?'

'I'm not going to California. My place is here with you and Virgil.'

'Are you crazy, boy!' Virgil yelled at him. 'You'll do what Wyatt and I say you will!'

James' face colored, and he looked away, avoiding Virgil's hard stare. 'You can send a note to Mattie with Morgan. I'll pay the freight handler to watch over Morgan's coffin on the trip west. We'll explain everything to Mattie in the note, and have her tell Warren to stay home.'

Wyatt saw that James had his chin stuck out, and smiled slightly. 'You're not a gunfighter, James. You wisely took a different path from Virgil and me. You think I'm going to let you ride with us and get yourself killed by one of those back-shooters? Haven't we had enough death in this family to last us a while?'

'Morgan was my brother, too!' James fairly shouted at him. 'I've been practicing, I can use a gun! If you won't take me with you, I'll stay here on my own. I want to see those murderers dead, if I have to do it myself!'

Doc looked over at Wyatt. 'It looks like he's staying, Wyatt.'

'The hell he is!' Virgil bellowed.

Wyatt sighed. 'No, wait, Virgil,' he said pensively. 'Maybe James has the right to stay on.'

Virgil glared at him. 'You're crazier than he is! You know the danger!'

'James and Morgan were very close,' Wyatt reminded him. 'I'll make him my responsibility. Let him ride with us, Virgil.'

Virgil's face slowly softened. Then he sighed heavily. 'With the three of you against me, what can I do?' He met James's bright look. 'But if you get yourself killed here in

Arizona, brother, you got me to answer to in the hereafter.'

James was grinning. 'I'll remember that, Virgil. And you won't be sorry. I'll make both of you proud of me.'

'Just try to stay alive,' Virgil advised him.

'That ought to be a big enough load to carry,' Doc commented drily.

It was a cold, damp morning the next day when they left town. James and Doc had gotten Morgan's pine coffin aboard a small, recently purchased wagon while the sky was still dark, and James's two brothers had arrived just as a mauve light was burgeoning in the eastern mountains. James and Doc had tethered their mounts to the rear of the wagon, and sat side by side on the buckboard behind the single dray horse that would pull the wagon.

They headed out at about 8.30, when the sky was brightening by the moment, with pencil-thin lines of red and gold streaking the horizon. Wyatt and Virgil rode alongside the wagon, flanking it, as it rumbled along Allen Street toward the town's edge. Doc and Wyatt both carried sawed-off American Arms 12-gauge shotguns across their laps, and Virgil rode with his gunhand resting lightly on his right-hand Peacemaker. As they passed the Union Market and the Grand Hotel, they found that a number of Clanton's ranch hands had gathered on the porches and balcony, and these men started hurling epithets at the small procession as it made its way out of town.

'Hey, look! There go the yellow-bellies!'

'Looks like the Clantons finally drove you murderers out!'

'Go on back to Kansas, Earps! While you still can!'

Wyatt rode alongside the wagon stoically. 'Leave it be,

Virgil,' he said to his brother, on the far side of the wagon.

'Had enough, huh? You black cowards!'

'Don't ever show your yellow bellies around here again! We won't let you ride out again!'

'Yeah, and bury that stinking corpse somewhere far away from here! We don't want no Earp smelling up the vicinity!'

James's face turned red. 'You dirty devils!' he shouted with a shaking voice. 'I wish you was all in hell with your backs broke!'

'Be quiet, James,' Wyatt said in a hard voice. 'Just drive the wagon.'

'Don't let those retards bother you, boy,' Doc told him. 'Most of them can't spell their own names.'

But then they left the town behind them and were out on the trail south. They heard some catcalls and jeering from behind them for a few moments, and then the silence of the desert crowded in. The only sounds were the horses' hoofs on the hard dirt, and the creaking of the wagon wheels.

'I have a feeling,' Wyatt commented as they moved along the bumpy trail, 'that that's not the end of it. They may not wait for us to regroup. They know this isn't over for us, and we're still a danger to them.'

'If they hit us, it will be an ambush,' Doc suggested, looking around him at the high Dragoon and Whetstone Mountains that flanked their route. 'They'll never attack us head on. We'd take too many of them with us before we went down.'

Wyatt was riding up alongside the buckboard, and James looked over at him, past Doc's thin profile. 'One of them lowlifes yelling at us was Frank Stilwell, Wyatt. J Did you see him?'

'I saw him,' Wyatt said grimly. 'That took some brass. To show his face after helping murder Morgan. Maybe Behan sent him out there, to show his feelings in this. Of course, he might not know yet that Stilwell was involved. If not, Ike Clanton will be happy to let him know. It's something Ike will have to hold over Behan's head.'

'Behan will just be another hired gun for the Clantons now,' Virgil surmised, from the other side of the wagon.

'And Ike will force Behan to do something to prove his loyalty,' Doc mused.

James whipped the dray horse around a pot-hole in the trail. He was dark-visaged. In the bed of the wagon the coffin bounced around, and James winced.

'I could have gunned him down right there, when we passed,' Virgil added, refering to Stilwell. 'And that much would be over.'

'You'd have drawn fire from every ranch hand lining the street,' Wyatt reminded him. 'And it's not just Stilwell who has to pay. We have to keep our heads now, and be smarter than they are.'

'Amen,' Doc put in.

In late afternoon they arrived at a fertile spot where two small rivers met, and encamped under a stand of cottonwoods. They were just over halfway to the town of Contention. Wyatt had noticed that Virgil was leaning forward in his saddle, and realized he was tiring because of his healing wounds, so ordered a halt where there would be water for them and the animals.

Nobody was talking now. Their heads were whirling with memories of the day, and the past few days. James unhitched the wagon mare, and helped Doc unsaddle the mounts and picket them to the trees while Wyatt and Virgil gathered firewood, built a low fire, and got some equipment off the wagon. Bedrolls were laid down, and Virgil opened a couple of tins of beans and set them on the fire, then threw some bacon into a frying pan. James built a spit over the fire, and they heated up some chicory coffee to wash the meal down. Virgil got some corn dodgers out of a meal bag, but only he tried to eat one. Partway through it, he threw the rest of it onto the ground.

'I think I cracked a tooth on that dinosaur egg,' he complained.

'I can fix that,' Doc commented. 'Let me tie a cord around the offending molar and I'll have it out before you get your meal digested.'

Virgil gave him a sour look. 'I think I'll hold on to it till I'm sure it's been damaged, Doc. If you don't mind.'

'I didn't bring my tools with me, or I could yank it out while you're waiting for that next pot of coffee to boil.'

'Too bad for me,' Virgil grimaced. But they had lightened the mood of the group.

They were sitting around the fire on saddles and logs. James was staring silently into the fire, and Wyatt was looking out into the growing darkness, wondering if this night would be an uneventful one for them. He set his tin plate down and sipped at his coffee.

'We'll stand watch tonight,' he announced. 'Two-hour shifts. Since you're all pretty tired, I'll take the first shift. Virgil, you ought to take the last one.'

'Is that really necessary?' James said with a frown. He had very little experience on the trail. 'We're all weary, Wyatt.'

'It's not just the Clantons,' Wyatt said. 'This trail is notorious for bandits. Travelers will ride to our fire. It's only one night. We ought to be pretty safe when we reach Contention.'

'I'll take second watch,' Doc volunteered. 'Anybody for more coffee?'

'Wait,' Wyatt said, holding his hand up. '1 think we might have company already.' Just over a close rise of ground came the quiet sound of hoofbeats.

They all stood up, setting their utensils on the ground. On the crest of the low hill not far from their camp were the silhouettes of three riders. The riders had reined in and were staring toward the campfire.

'It must be Clanton men!' James whispered harshly.

Wyatt shook his head. 'I don't think so. The Clantons are ambushers, and we're out in the open here. Look, they're walking their mounts on down to us. Keep your iron holstered.'

'Are you sure?' James asked breathlessly.

'Just listen to your brother, boy,' Doc told him.

The riders came on into the light of their fire, and stopped a few yards away. They were shoddily dressed, motley-looking men, all three big and husky, and all carried big revolvers prominently on their belts.

'Drifters,' Doc said quietly to Virgil, standing beside him.

One of the drifters' horses guffered quietly, and the man in the middle, who was a bit taller than the others, leaned on his saddle horn and grinned. 'Evening, boys. Hope we ain't disturbing your quiet none. We saw your fire, and thought maybe you had enough coffee to share with us weary riders.'

Wyatt looked them over carefully. 'We can give you one cup. Come on in. There's water for your horses at the stream.'

James gave him a curious look.

'Much obliged,' a second rider grunted out. Even in

this light, they could see that part of his left ear was gone, with a thick scar there.

'Yeah, we sure are thirsty,' the third one spoke up as they all dismounted. His hair was longer than that of his companions, falling onto his shoulders, and had a dirty, stringy look.

They all walked up to the fire, and they were tough-looking men. They left their horses where they reined them in, making no effort to water them. Wyatt emptied coffee cups and poured fresh coffee for them while his brothers and Doc watched the newcomers carefully. Everybody was still standing. Doc gestured toward the seats around the fire.

'Take some weight off, boys.'

The tall one who had spoken first shook his head. He was unshaven, and the neckerchief at his throat looked soiled. 'No, thanks, I think we'll stand, boys.'

'Suit yourselves,' Virgil told them.

The three of them sipped at their coffee cups, and stared at the Earp party over the rims. Bad Ear gave Longhair a casual look, as the tall one addressed Virgil nearest him. 'You boys are dressed mighty fancy, with them pretty coats and ties. You must be city boys.'

James looked quickly toward Virgil, then Wyatt, to see their reactions. They and Doc still wore their dark suits, lariat ties and black hats, with long gray riding-coats over the suits. James wore the more traditional work trousers, and a sheepskin jacket over a corduroy vest.

'We just came from Tombstone,' Virgil said.

'Oh, sure,' Bad Ear grinned. 'You must be gamblers. Right?'

Wyatt quickly intervened. 'We did some gambling there.' The guns of the Earp party were still pretty well hidden by their riding-coats.

'I don't like gamblers,' Longhair said in an off-hand way. 'No offense.'

'I shot one in the belly in Albuquerque,' Bad Ear blurted out, laughing a guttural laugh. He swigged the rest of his coffee and then deliberately threw the tin cup onto the ground, staring at Virgil as he did so.

'I see you're carrying something in the wagon,' the tall man said. 'What you got in that big box?'

'That's our business,' James responded.

'It's personal,' Wyatt added smoothly.

'Personal?' the tall fellow said, looking Wyatt up and down.' 'What do you mean, personal?'

'He means personal,' Virgil said in a hard voice. 'Now, if you boys are finished with our coffee, you might want to get back on those mounts and be on your way. We have bedding to make up.'

The tall one arched his dark brow. 'Whoa, there. We ain't hardly got our riding kinks out yet. To tell you the truth, I don't like it much that you won't reveal the contents of that box. What else you hauling on that wagon?'

'It's nothing of interest to you,' Wyatt said.

The tall man looked him over again. 'I was asking that boy over there.'

Doc shook his head slowly. 'You ought to be thankful he's talking to you at all, boys.'

The threesome all looked over at Doc, who had just moved closer to the fire. Longhair stared hard at him. 'You look like you just crawled out of the ground somewhere, mister.'

'Is that right?' Doc said in a soft, sibilant voice.

The tall fellow rested his hand on a big revolver on his

hip. 'Maybe we better decide whether that cargo is interesting to us. What do you think of that, fancy Dans?'

'You three are out of your minds!' James put in hotly.

But then Virgil also stepped forward. 'Do you boys have any idea who you're talking to?' he said easily.

'Sure,' Bad Ear spoke up. 'Three candy-ass card sharps and a fuzz-faced loud-mouth. Do I get a cigar?'

Virgil ignored the insults. 'This here by the fire is Doc Holliday.'

Doc pushed his riding coat aside and revealed the two big Peacemakers hanging low on his hips.

'And that other fancy Dan over there is Wyatt Earp,' Virgil added.

Wyatt eased back his long coat and his under-coat too. His two bone-handled revolvers shone in the firelight.

'And we're Wyatt's brothers, Virgil and James,' Virgil concluded. 'Now, you trio of widow-robbers. You still want to look in that wagon?'

Bad Ear swallowed hard, and studied the men before him. He hadn't noticed their faces before. Not really. The steely eyes. The set of their chins. He cast a scared look at the tall fellow, who had quickly removed his hand from his gun.

'You're the Earps? And Doc Holliday?'

'Sure,' Longhair remarked caustically. 'And I'm Buffalo Bill.'

'Shut up, Joey,' the tall man said, his voice tight. 'You're the Earps from Dodge City?'

'The same,' Virgil told them.

Bad Ear glanced over toward Doc. 'Doc Holliday. You're the fastest gun west of the Mississippi.'

Doc shook his head. 'Not quite. He is.' He gestured toward Wyatt.

Now the tall man swallowed. Suddenly the guns on the other side looked as big as cannons. 'We didn't know.'

'And that makes it right?' Wyatt growled out.

Longhair was convinced now, too. 'I'm not drawing. I'm throwing down.' He reached slowly, drew his revolver and dropped it into the dirt beside the fire. Wyatt shook his head slowly.

'Well, you had your coffee,' Wyatt said. 'I guess you'll be wanting to ride out now.'

'We heard something about a gunfight in Tombstone. You boys killed some Clantons.'

'Just one,' Virgil corrected him. 'The others were McLaurys.'

'Ike Clanton wants some hired guns. We was riding there to answer the call. Was that because of his fight with you boys?'

'What do you think?' James said.

The threesome exchanged dark looks. 'Well, we don't want no part of this,' the tall fellow said. 'I reckon we'll be riding back to Albuquerque.'

'That might extend your longevity,' Doc suggested acidly.

'Well. We'll be riding on out. Sorry about this.'

'Try to find an honest way to make a living,' Wyatt advised.

Bad Ear stepped forward. 'Say, Mr Earp. Mind if I ask for your autograph? I got a pencil in my saddle-bags.'

Wyatt looked angry for the first time. 'Get to hell out of here,' he said flatly. 'Before I really lose my temper.'

Bad Ear nodded jerkily. 'Yes, sir. No offense.'

A moment later they had ridden back out, heading in the same direction as they had come.

'They're the kind that usually find more trouble than

they can handle,' Doc offered as he poured himself a last cup of boiling-hot chicory.

The four seated themselves around the fire again. Doc sipped at the coffee, burning his mouth.

'I'm glad we didn't have to kill them,' Virgil grunted out.

'Maybe we should have,' Doc suggested. 'They still might end up at the Clanton ranch.'

'I don't think so,' Wyatt said. 'I watched their eyes. They were scared.'

'They sure ought to be!' James blustered.

Wyatt smiled in the firelight. 'Virgil, when did we get that wire from Warren?'

'Oh, just a couple days ago. When our little brother heard about the shoot-out at the Corral, he told Allie he was coming straight back here. He thinks we need him.' A sardonic grin.

'The kid knows nothing about guns!' James said with a scowl.

'Neither do you,' Virgil retorted, grimacing when he moved his healing arm.

James gave him a dark look, and Doc grunted out a quiet laugh.

'His stopping-off place would be Contention,' Wyatt said. 'He might already be there by now. And he won't know we're headed there with Morgan.'

'Well, we'll know all about that tomorrow,' Doc reminded them. 'I say we play some cards and go to bed.'

'Cards?' James said tiredly. 'You must be crazy, Doc. I'm just going to lay my head down on my bedroll and get some sleep. If I can, with Morgan over there on that wagon.'

'I think James has the best idea, Doc,' Wyatt told him.

'We have a long day tomorrow. You three go on to bed, and I'll take first watch. James, you can spell me, and then Doc can take over from you. Virgil can wake us up just before dawn.'

There were a couple of nods, and they rose and went to their bedrolls. They seldom questioned Wyatt's decisions. Even Doc recognized him as their natural leader.

In an hour they were all asleep except Wyatt. He sat beside the guttering fire, staring at a yellow moon rising over a nearby hill like the harbinger of a cataclysm, in its bold intensity. Wyatt found himself wondering what his world might be like by the time that cosmic orb returned to this place on its monthly journey.

A coyote wailed out its nocturnal song, out there on the plain somewhere. He listened to it carefully, to try to understand its message to the silent hills.

One thing was certain. He would not be leaving these hills alive until three killers of his brother were dead.

That much was written in the Arizona sand.

CHAPTER FIVE

The night passed uneventfully. On James's watch, there was sheet lightning over in the west, but no storm ever reached them. They were all up and having morning coffee by sunrise. Virgil's arm had stiffened up, and Doc looked as if he had sat up out of a coffin. But with three cups of coffee, some color came into his sallow face. It always took James a long time to wake up, and he barely spoke a word as they packed their gear up and prepared to set out on the trail again. Wyatt took charge, assigning tasks and getting things done. As James rolled his bed up, Wyatt saw his gunbelt still lying close beside it.

'I told you, James. Always re-arm yourself before anything else.'

'Oh, for God's sake, Wyatt.'

'Then you can help Virgil with his bed. I heard him moaning from that side wound last night.'

'I don't need no nursemaiding, Wyatt,' Virgil growled.

Wyatt turned a cool stare on him. He was in a sour mood, waking up in the small hours with the killers of Morgan on his mind. 'I don't want to have to deal with stubborn back-talk this morning, Virgil. You let James roll that bed up.'

Virgil saw the look on Wyatt's face, and his countenance softened. 'All right, Grandma. Just as you say.'

'Let's get riding,' Doc complained. 'The damp got right into my bones last night.'

The riding was easy that day. It was mostly open country, but they passed a big ranch where a small herd of longhorns was crowded up against a butte, chewing their cuds into the wind. These were the kind of ranches Ike Clanton preyed upon from his place outside of Tombstone. That activity had been sharply curtailed since the arrival of the Earps, but this type of outlawry had already come to the attention of the federal government in Washington, and President Chester Arthur was considering the appointment of new federal marshals throughout the Southwest, and also threatened to call out the army to stop the rampant rustling. Ike Clanton's days were numbered, and the Earps would no longer be needed in Tombstone. Wyatt had no plans to return there to wear a badge again. But he wouldn't leave Arizona until Morgan's death had been answered.

It was just after noon when they arrived in Contention.

It was a rather small cattle town, with all the businesses on one long street. The railroad came right through the center of town, where there was a small depot. Behind the depot was a stockyard where cattle waited to be shipped off to points east and west. As they arrived in town there was a lot of carriage and pedestrian traffic on the streets, and business was bustling. They pulled their wagon bearing Morgan's body up to a small hotel short of the train station. A couple of young women with parasols came out of the place and sauntered down the boardwalk past their wagon. They gave their group a disdainful glance.

'Hey, this looks like a real civilized place,' James observed.

Wyatt was looking around for any sign of Ike Clanton or his men. 'Looks can be deceiving, James,' he commented. 'We better go inside and get us a couple rooms for the night. The train west doesn't leave until early tomorrow.'

'I'll take the wagon on down to the hostelry,' James offered, as Virgil climbed down off the wagon seat. Wyatt and Doc dismounted and tethered their horses to a hitching rail.

'We'll meet you in the lobby,' Wyatt told him. He took a small leather poke from his saddle-bag and handed it to James. There was the jingle of gold coins inside. 'Here. Give this to the hostler to keep a close watch over Morgan.'

James nodded. 'It might help. He's beginning to smell a little.'

Wyatt started to reply to that when he saw Virgil staring at the open doorway to the hotel, where a young man was emerging. 'Well, if this don't beat all!'

They all looked toward the doorway, and saw Warren Earp standing there with wide eyes, having just seen them. Wyatt's face went very sober. He had hoped Warren would stay home.

'Virgil! Wyatt, James! It's a miracle!'

'I'll be damned,' Wyatt said quietly.

Warren hurried down the steps to ground level as James climbed down from the wagon. 'Warren! It's really you!'

Warren came and threw himself onto Wyatt, knocking him up against the wagon, giving him a big bear-hug. 'Damn, Wyatt!'

'Whoa, boy.' Wyatt grinned. 'Take it slow.'

Warren turned to hug Virgil as James came around the

wagon. Then he noticed Virgil's arm sling. 'Hey. You're hurt.' He was dressed like a Boston store clerk, with a tight vest and bow tie, and he wore a derby hat. He looked a lot like James, but slimmer and more innocent-looking. James was the oldest and he the youngest of the brothers. Neither of them knew about guns. Under the hat was a thick shock of auburn hair, which gave him a different look from his dark-haired brothers.

'It's nothing serious, Bubba,' Virgil told him as James arrived. He had always called Warren by that pet name, even though the other brothers had never adopted it.

'Hey, kid!' James exclaimed. 'You're looking just great!'

'Wow. You boys look rich.' Warren grinned.

'This here is Doc Holliday,' Wyatt said.

Warren extended his hand. 'I've heard a lot about you, Doc. The pleasure is all mine.'

Doc took his hand in a limp grasp, and stifled a cough. 'Glad to make your acquaintance, Warren. Any Earp is a friend of mine.'

Warren found himself glancing down at Doc's big guns. 'Any friend to my brothers is my friend, too.' He looked toward the wagon for the first time. 'Say, what are you boys doing here at Contention? I thought I'd have to ride clear up to Tombstone on horseback. And what's in that wagon? You selling off some of Wyatt's gambling equipment?'

All of the other faces went somber. Virgil glanced over at Wyatt, and Wyatt gave a small sigh. 'The folks back home know this already, Warren. You left before the news came. Morgan was murdered in Tombstone. That's him in the wagon there.'

'Oh, God,' Warren gasped out. 'Oh, my God.'

He walked up to the wagon, and stared down at the coffin. He just stood there silent for a long moment. When he turned back, his cheeks were moist. 'Who did this, Wyatt?'

'It was Ike Clanton's men,' Wyatt said. 'They back-shot him. Don't worry, kid. We're taking care of it.'

'We're shipping him off to California tomorrow morning,' Virgil said.

'And Virgil's accompanying him home,' Wyatt added firmly. It had been a big argument to get Virgil to leave Arizona.

Virgil gave him a hurt look. 'Yeah. I'll be going, too. You ought to turn right around and go home with me, Bubba. You're not needed out here.'

'I didn't come all the way out here to turn around and go home!' Warren said loudly. 'I want to be in on this! Morgan was my brother, too!'

'You don't even carry a gun,' James said evenly. 'Your place is at home, to help bury Morgan and comfort Louisa and the women.'

'You go comfort the women!' Warren said emotionally. 'And I'll say where my place is, James! Not you. Not even Wyatt!'

'Why don't we go inside and have us some grub at the hotel restaurant?' Doc said easily. 'This isn't street talk.'

'Doc's right,' Wyatt said solemnly, clapping a hand onto Warren's shoulder. 'Come on, little brother. We'll all feel better after a nice meal. James, you go on down to the hostler, and we'll order you something.'

A few moments later James was driving the wagon down the street, and the other four men were registering at the hotel desk. Then they went into a rather small restaurant off the lobby and ordered five steaks. By the time their orders came, James had returned, and they all ate silently together. Partway through the meal, Virgil broke the silence.

'How are things going in your store business back home, Bubba? You look like you're doing pretty well.' He glanced at Warren's vest.

'Things are fine back there,' Warren replied, looking a bit sullen. 'All your wives sent their love. Mattie said to tell Wyatt to take that badge off and come home.' He looked up ruefully. 'Before somebody gets killed.'

A heavy silence fell back over the table as they all thought of Morgan. Then Wyatt after some moments spoke. 'We already quit the law,' he said quietly. 'But we have a job to do here before we can go home.'

Warren held his gaze. 'I want to be a part of that,' he said firmly.

They had all finished eating now. Doc and Virgil were sipping at beer glasses. Wyatt touched his mouth with a napkin. 'When was the last time you fired a gun, little brother? A year ago? More?'

Warren averted his look. 'I practiced some before I came out here. I thought I'd buy a piece in Tombstone. I didn't figure I'd need one on the train.'

James shook his head. 'Warren, you should have stayed home. You don't have the kind of experience needed to deal with gunslingers.'

'How much do you have?' Warren responded, his young face flushed. 'You been tending bar out here.'

Beefy Virgil grinned slightly. 'He has a point, James.'

Doc pulled a big revolver from his left-hand holster, flipped it over, and handed it over to Warren. 'Take it, kid.'

Warren hesitated, then grabbed the butt of the hefty gun.

Doc turned in his chair. 'See that Wanted dodger on the back wall there?'

77

They all looked back there. It was a poster announcing a small reward for the apprehension of a local, small-time thief. The suspect's picture was shown on the center of the poster.

'See if you can hit that boy in the head,' Doc suggested.

James issued a small, grunting laugh. Wyatt watched Warren's face, as Virgil intervened. 'That's all right, Warren. You don't have to prove anything.'

'Let him shoot,' Wyatt said evenly.

Warren gave Wyatt a quick glance, then without further hesitation turned, aimed, and fired. The big gun's explosion shook the rafters of the dining room and made their ears ring. When the smoke cleared, there was a hole in the nose of the pictured thief.

Virgil whistled through his teeth, and James's eyes went wide.

'Hey! No shooting in here, boys!' A cry came from a fat proprietor at the door to the kitchen.

Warren turned back to them with a satisfied grin. 'Nice balance, Doc. I think I'll get me one like that.'

Doc took the gun back with a similar grin. 'Good shooting, boy.'

'I don't believe it,' James said hollowly.

Virgil looked over at Wyatt. 'It looks like he's staying.'

Wyatt nodded, his eyes studying Warren's young face. 'It looks that way.'

Warren's face brightened. 'Thanks, Wyatt.'

'Don't thank me, kid. You just stepped into a pile of cow dung. You have to know more than how to shoot a poster picture to handle men like John Ringo and Pete Spence. You have a lot to learn, and if you don't know that, you could end up like Morgan. And that would be on me.'

'I won't let you down, Wyatt,' Warren said with big eyes.

'I swear it.'

'We'll see,' Wyatt said soberly. 'Now, let's go see what those rooms look like.'

That afternoon was largely spent bringing Warren up to date on happenings since the gunfight at the OK Corral, while Doc walked down to the nearest saloon and made almost $200 playing one eyed jacks. Everybody went to bed early in the evening, after Wyatt walked down to check on Morgan.

By nine the next morning they were all down at the railroad depot waiting for the train that would take Morgan an Virgil back to California. Virgil and Doc were now quite relaxed about possible trouble, but Wyatt was always watching his close surroundings. He knew Ike Clanton probably wouldn't be satisfied with the Earps' merely leaving Tombstone now. It had gone beyond that. If he found an opportunity to kill Wyatt and Virgil, he would take it. Then he wouldn't have to worry over where they were, and whether they were returning for revenge.

The train grunted and lumbered into town at 9.28, two minutes ahead of its scheduled arrival, gushing steam and belching smoke. Wyatt and James had unloaded Morgan from the wagon out front, and brought the coffin onto the platform on a cart, and it was ready for loading. There were three passenger cars up front, and then five freight cars behind. The station master came up to Virgil shortly after the locomotive ground to a shrieking stop.

'Is this the body you're shipping to California?'

'That's right,' Virgil told him. 'It's going all the way to Colton. I'll be accompanying it in third class.'

'OK. You got a separate ticket for the box?'

'Right here,' Wyatt told him, proffering a small piece of paper.

'All right, let's get it aboard. I hope it don't stink up the whole car.'

Wyatt grabbed the man's arm and turned him around. 'That's our brother you're talking about, mister. Have a little respect.'

The station master swallowed hard, and looked down at his Peacemakers. 'Say. It says Earp on that slip. You wouldn't be Wyatt, I guess?'

'Why wouldn't I be?' Wyatt said in a hard voice.

'Oh, nothing, Mr Earp. No offense intended. We'll take real good care of your brother. I'll give special instructions.'

'Be sure you do,' James put in.

A few minutes later the box was on board, and they all walked back to the passenger car where Virgil would be riding.

'You boys take a minute,' Doc said then. 'I'll just go inside and look at train schedules while you say your goodbyes.'

After he was gone, Wyatt turned to Virgil, whose arm was still in a sling. 'Sorry you can't be here for the rest of it, Virgil. But you did your part. It's more important you take care of Morgan now. And get him a proper burial.'

Virgil sighed. He had been the town marshal at Tombstone, with the ultimate responsibility to uphold the law. It was almost too much to bear, to leave now before it was over. But he realized he was in no shape to fight.

'I understand, Wyatt. But listen to me. I'm leaving James and Warren in your care. Try to keep them safe as long as you can.'

'I will.'

'We can take care of ourselves, Virgil,' James said.

Virgil's face clouded over. 'You know, you've lived long

enough to have got some sense, James,' he said harshly. 'You don't have the same excuse as little Bubba. You think because you been wearing a gun, you can handle yourself. But you've never had to answer to men like Ike's put together. You listen to Wyatt. He can tell you things, if you'll just pay attention. And Doc. He knows it all. You hear me?'

James nodded slowly. 'I get it, Virgil.'

'I hardly got to talk to you,' Warren said, his voice breaking. He came over and hugged Virgil, making him grimace in pain. 'There's a good doctor in Colton. You have him tend that wound. He'll make you well.'

Virgil grinned behind his mustache. 'I'll do that, Bubba. Now, keep your head low and don't try to be a hero. Leave that to Wyatt.' He gave Wyatt a bigger grin.

'We'll be all right,' Warren assured him.

'Listen brother,' Wyatt said quietly then. 'Tell Mattie I'm through with lawing. As soon as we've made things right here, we'll all be back home.'

'I'll be sure to do that, Wyatt,' Virgil replied. His eyes moistened slightly. At the front of the train, the whistle blew, announcing an imminent departure. 'Well, I'll be getting aboard. At least I'll have Morgan with me.'

'Have a good trip,' James told him.

Virgil's and Wyatt's eyes locked for a moment, then he was gone inside the train.

'All aboard!' the station master called out.

A moment later the train chugged away from the station, filling the air with black smoke. The three brothers stared after it as it slowly disappeared down the tracks, rolling west.

'At least two of us are headed home,' James said.

As they turned to make their way through the depot to

the street, the station master walked over to them with a smile. He addressed himself to Wyatt.

'Well, I see your brother got himself aboard all right, Mr Earp,' he said. 'It will be good to have someone aboard to watch over the coffin on its arrival in Colton.'

'Yes, that's right,' Wyatt replied curtly. 'Now, if you'll excuse us.'

'Oh, I almost forgot. Did your friends find you all right?'

Wyatt stopped, and frowned at him. 'What friends?'

'Why, the ones that was asking about you last night here at the depot.'

James gave Wyatt a dark look. Warren merely looked curious.

'I thought they would've found you by now,' the railroad man continued. 'They asked me if some men had arrived with a coffin to put aboard the train. They wanted to offer their respects.'

Wyatt's face had hardened, and his piercing blue eyes bored into the other man. 'What did these men look like, and how many were there?'

The station master, a middle-aged fellow with graying hair, took his cap off and scratched his head, thinking. 'Goodness. I think there was three of them. Dressed like ranchers. Of course, I didn't know about your shipment then. But I heard them talking among themselves, and I'm pretty sure your name was mentioned. I heard them say 'Earp' pretty plain.'

'It's Ike's people,' Wyatt said softly. 'Did they ask when the next train was leaving for California?'

'I don't think so. But you know, I think I saw one of them studying our schedule posted on the depot wall.' He hesitated, and his eyes widened slightly. 'Oh, my! That schedule has been changed. Why, I should've told them, Mr Earp! Your train left almost an hour earlier than they thought! I'm real sorry, that's why they missed you here!'

'My God,' James muttered.

'What?' Warren frowned.

'They'll probably still be here, if you want to wait a little for them,' the station master went on blithely. Wyatt's eyes were already scanning the doorways of the depot. 'But you can leave a message with me if you'd like. I kind of feel like it's all my fault. Why don't—'

In the next moment the morning erupted in a cacophony of raucous gunfire, coming from both ends of the depot building. The first shot struck the station master, who was standing close to Wyatt. Hit in the lower back, he was thrown up against Wyatt, where another chunk of lead slammed into his side.

The gunfire was deafening. It was coming from three shooters, two of them at the far corner of the building, and one at the near corner. They all wore masks, but were dressed like ranch hands.

As Wyatt drew both Peacemakers, he was struck a grazing hit on the left side, under his ribs, and James was hit in the left arm. Unarmed Warren had ducked low into a crouch, and wasn't hit. Other bullets caromed off a platform cart behind Wyatt, and the tracks beyond.

Now Wyatt was returning deadly fire with both guns toward the two men at the far end of the depot. One was hit in center chest and then the belly, and the second one took a grazing hit to the thigh. James had returned fire to the third assailant, but missed. There were a couple more shots from both directions, then the two remaining ambushers fled. Wyatt felt some crimson on his vest and shirt, but the wound was shallow. Acrid, pungent gunsmoke filled the air around him.

'Are you two all right?' he said to his brothers.

Warren had come out of his crouch, unscathed, and James was examining his left arm. 'It's just a scratch, Wyatt.'

Wyatt looked down at the station master as Doc emerged from the depot, gun drawn. 'What happened? I was having a coughing fit inside.'

'We were ambushed,' Wyatt said. 'I think one of them that ran off was Ike Clanton.'

There was the sound of hoofbeats receding down the street, on the other side of the depot. 'That's them,' Wyatt said. 'We'll never catch them.'

James knelt over the station master. 'He's still alive, Wyatt.'

'Good. You and Warren get him inside, and yell for a doctor. Come with me, Doc.'

They walked down to the end of the building, where the gunman had fallen. Wyatt knelt over him and took a bandanna off his face.

'Well, what do you know,' Doc said. 'That low life Frank Stilwell.'

'One of the three that gunned down Morgan,' Wyatt said. 'Good. Just two to go.'

James came walking up to them. 'Warren and the ticket man took the station master down the street a couple doors to a doctor. My God. It's Stilwell.'

'The same,' Wyatt said. 'Did we gather quite a crowd out there?'

'Not bad. There was nobody in the waiting room. A few pedestrians from the street are gathered out there. Warren walked right past them. He'll be on his way back any minute. What do you want to do?'

'I was going to sell the wagon today. But I think we might better ride right out of here. We don't know this town marshal. Ike might have him in his back pocket. We're heading back to Tombstone.'

Both Doc and James eyed him somberly.

'Back into the eye of the storm?' Doc said.

'Maybe that's where it's safest,' Wyatt told them. 'I know a fellow owns a cabin a few miles east of town. I don't think Ike knows about him. His name is Sherman McMasters. He hates the Clantons. He'll take us in.'

'Look,' James said. 'Here comes Warren.'

'Then we're ready to ride out,' Wyatt told him.

CHAPTER SIX

It had been a wild day, Wyatt reminisced, that cool
October morning at the OK Corral. Even wilder than what
had just happened in Contention. Wyatt had been
involved in most of it, and had had the rest reported to
him by reliable witnesses. It all started at about 1.00 a.m.,
in the Alhambra saloon, where Ike Clanton had gone for
a light, late-night meal. Wyatt happened to be there
eating, too, and brother Morgan was behind the bar,
talking to the bartender. Ike almost left when he saw
Wyatt, but sat down and ordered his food. A moment later
Doc Holliday walked in, to join Wyatt at a meal. He had
been drinking. As soon as he spotted Ike, he strode over
to his table.

'You sonofabitch of a rustler, go for your iron!'

Ike stuck his lantern jaw out and regarded Doc with
hard eyes. 'I'm not carrying,' he said evenly. 'Look for
yourself.'

Doc drew his left-hand Peacemaker. 'Here, damn you!
Now you don't have any excuse, you piece of cow dung!
Take it up or I'll shoot you down like the dirty dog you are!'

'Morgan,' Wyatt said easily, forking up another piece of
steak.

Morgan nodded, and went and grabbed Doc's arm. 'Come on, Doc. Take it outside. You're in a lunch room.'

Doc tore his arm from Morgan's grasp. 'You mean to tell Doc Holliday to vacate this rat-trap of a grub house?'

'No,' Morgan said quietly. 'Wyatt does.'

Doc turned toward Wyatt as if he had seen him for the first time. He just stood there for a moment, getting himself under control, while Ike watched him carefully. Wyatt glanced over at him.

'Evening, Doc. Why don't you go on down the street to the Oriental with Morgan and cool off? I'll join you there as soon as I finish this steak.'

Doc ran a hand over his mouth, cooling down some. He gave Ike a brittle glance, then lifted his rheumy eyes to Wyatt. 'I accept that invitation, Wyatt. As for you, you snake in the grass,' to Ike, 'I recommend you arm yourself.'

Doc left with Morgan then, and Wyatt finished his meal. But the day was just beginning for all of them.

Those thoughts were running through Wyatt's head like bats in a cave as he, his two brothers and Doc rode north toward Tombstone that afternoon after the shoot-out in Contention. Wyatt had been right. Ike had no intention of letting the Earps just leave for Calfifornia as long as he had it in his power to stop them. Now it would be a small war, until Wyatt had made Morgan's murder right.

Even in southern Arizona the March day was a cool one when they headed back toward Tombstone. Wyatt and Doc rode side by side, and James and Warren followed along behind them. Wyatt decided to camp at the same site they had used on the way to Contention, and by late afternoon they were there. Warren and James noticed how quiet

Wyatt had been on the trail, and after they got settled in and were chowing down around a low fire, Warren mentioned Wyatt's silence.

'Is everything all right, brother?' he asked as they sipped at their chicory coffee after a light meal. 'You've been real quiet.'

'He's always quiet,' James put in.

'He's thinking of how we came to all this,' Doc said, without looking up.

Wyatt glanced over at him. 'You just have to think it could have been avoided. All of it.'

'Not when you're dealing with a damn rattlesnake like Ike,' Doc said. 'You know there was no choice in this, Wyatt.'

'We didn't get much news of it back home,' Warren said. 'It sounds like that corral fight was pretty inevitable, though.'

Wyatt stared out over the prairie as night fell over their camp. After that confrontation at the Alhambra, Ike had gone to Hatch's poolroom and played cards all night with some cronies, while the embarrassment Doc had caused him at the Alhambra festered within him. By late morning he was bleary-eyed from lack of sleep, and in a foul mood.

'Ned Boyle woke me up at about 11.30,' Wyatt said pensively, talking more to himself than to them. 'He said he just spoke to Ike on the street, and Ike told him: "As soon as them damn Earps make their appearence outside today, the street will be filled with gunsmoke".'

That summary was followed by a heavy silence. Eventually James spoke up. 'Not much later Virgil spotted Ike loitering in an alley with a rifle, and took it away from him. Ike told him that if he'd seen him coming, he'd have shot him dead.'

'But that wasn't the end of it,' Warren said.

'No,' Wyatt told him. He was talking more about that day than he ever had since. 'Ike was heard saying he wanted to find me, to kill me. I found him down by the courthouse at about noon, and told him the threats had to stop, that I was an officer of the law. He said it would stop when it was over, and that might be later that day.' He shook his head slowly.

'Tom McLaury met Wyatt in the street shortly after that,' James continued the story. 'He said he'd make a fight with Wyatt anywhere he wanted. Wyatt disarmed him and told him to go home.'

'But they didn't,' Warren surmised, sipping at his coffee.

The campfire crackled loudly for a moment, and a cool wind rose across the plains.

'That's right,' James went on, knowing that Wyatt really didn't want to talk much about it. 'Suddenly Billy Clanton and Frank McLaury appeared in town on a freight wagon, not knowing what had happened. But when they talked to Ike and Tom, the whole mood of the day changed. Billy was telling Ike that they had to do something about the Earps, and the time was ripe. So they sent Sheriff Behan to tell the Earps that they were not leaving town and they were not going to be disarmed, and the Earps could do what they wanted about it. Behan said to let him handle them, but Virgil was town marshal, and it was the Earps' responsibility to keep order in Tombstone.'

'That's enough, James,' Wyatt said quietly.

'No, please, Wyatt,' Warren pleaded. 'This may be my only chance to hear the whole story.'

James looked at Wyatt and Wyatt reluctantly gave permission with his eyes.

'Well. I'll shorten this up,' James said, letting a long breath out. 'Wyatt, Virgil and Morgan went down to the corral area where the Clantons and McLaurys were gathered, just to disarm them. Doc here volunteered as a deputy despite Wyatt's protests. Right, Doc?'

Doc sighed heavily. 'I knew those boys were out for blood. Wyatt was my friend, what could I do?'

Wyatt looked over at him and smiled tiredly.

'When Virgil and his deputies reached the corral, Virgil ordered the ranchers to throw down their guns,' James went on. 'I saw the whole thing. Ike and Frank McLaury replied by cocking their revolvers. Billy drew and leveled his revolver at Wyatt. But Wyatt ignored that threat and fired on Frank, who had also drawn. Billy missed Wyatt but Wyatt shot Frank. Then Morgan hit Billy in the chest, and he went down, too. Tom McLaury threw his gun down and hid behind a horse.

'Afraid to draw on Wyatt, Ike lunged at him, but Wyatt knocked him to the ground, inviting him to draw. When Wyatt's attention was drawn then to Billy, Ike got up and ran off, hiding in a Mexican dance hall on Allen Street. Then the horse Tom was hiding behind bolted and Doc, seeing him, rearmed, fired and hit him in the side, which later killed him. Billy was far from out of the fight, and now fired and hit Virgil in the lower leg. Frank McLaury then fired at and hit Doc in the hip, and Morgan returned fire and hit Frank in the head, finishing him off. And finally, the dying Billy fired and hit Morgan in the shoulder, and Wyatt and Morgan returned fire together, both hitting Billy again and killing him.'

'And that was the end of it,' Doc said, coughing up some sputum. 'I still have to use a cane now and then from that bullet in my hip.'

'My God,' Warren said hollowly, trying to cram all of that summary into his head.

'It was all over in less than sixty seconds,' Doc said. 'Three men dead, three wounded. Wyatt wasn't even scratched, and Ike ran off without being hit.'

'I should have shot Ike when he lunged at me,' Wyatt said pensively. 'Then it would have been finished.'

The group fell into silence then for a long time, until, at last, Wyatt broke it. 'Morgan would still be alive.'

'Ike Clanton would have demanded revenge,' Doc said after a moment. 'Nobody can say how it would have ended.'

Wyatt slid his hand under his coat, where there was a light bandage now on his side. There was a crimson stain on his shirt there. 'Well, at least the ambush at Contention got something done that had to happen. Frank Stilwell is dead. Now there's just two left that murdered Morgan. Pete Spence and Indian Charlie.'

'They're both dangerous,' Doc said, laying his tin cup on the ground beside him. 'Spence is as good with a gun as Ringo, and Charlie is a wild man. They say he can hear somebody coming up on him from a half-mile away. And I doubt we'll catch them off by themselves. Also, when Ike figures out we're still here, he'll get Behan to form a posse to come after us. We did kill one of Morgan's murderers, after all.'

James and Warren were looking a little uncomfortable, and Wyatt saw the fear in their faces. 'Don't worry, brothers. You'll probably never hear the shot that kills you.'

James saw the small grin on Wyatt's face, and gave him a sour look. 'Very funny, brother.'

But Wyatt wasn't really joking, and he was now

regretting allowing James and Warren to acompany him. He had already lost one brother to his own bad judgment, he figured.

He didn't know what he would do if he lost another.

It was almost midday on the following day when the Earp party rode up to the McMasters cabin. They had watched the hills and trees around them all the way there, hoping to avoid another ambush. But Ike Clanton had no idea yet that they were back, and their arrival was peaceful.

The cabin was a sizeable one, sitting on a small stream with a hillside behind it. It was a log-and-mortar structure, with windows that had translucent hides stretched over them to allow light in. There was a heavy front door with leather hinges. McMasters had built the place himself, not long after his arrival in the area. He had come to Tombstone to gamble for a living, but found he liked the outdoors, and had turned to hunting and trapping lately. McMasters had met Wyatt and James at the Oriental saloon on a number of occasions. He had a rancher cousin in southern Arizona whose cattle had been rustled a while back by Ike Clanton, but there hadn't been enough hard evidence against Ike to bring him to court. McMasters had recently called Ike some names to his face, at the Alhambra, and Ike had threatened him. McMasters had also told Wyatt that if he ever needed another deputy to go against Ike, he was available.

By the time the foursome had dismounted and hitched their mounts to a rail at the front of the cabin, the door opened and McMasters stood there holding a sawed-off eight-gauge shotgun.

'Who's there?' he called out at the door. Then he recognized Wyatt. 'Well, I'll be hogtied! It's Marshal Earp!'

They walked up to the door, and he set the shotgun against the doorjamb. Wyatt extended his hand. 'Good to see you again, Sherman. I think you know my brother James, and Doc Holliday. This gawky-looking kid over here is my youngest brother, Warren. Fresh from California.'

'Nice to see you again, James, Doc. And right pleasured to meet up with you, Warren. I always wanted to get out to California.' He turned back to Wyatt. 'I thought you must be gone off somewhere by now, Wyatt. Maybe to California to bury Morgan.'

'No, Virgil is taking care of that,' Wyatt told him. 'We've still got business here to attend to. Mind if we come in and talk a little?'

McMasters invited them all inside and they were served real coffee, boiling-hot from the fireplace kettle. They all sat around a big dining table and relaxed, not talking business for a few minutes. Then Wyatt broached the subject.

'Sherman, I'm here to kill Pete Spence and Indian Charlie.'

McMasters stared hard at him. 'They work for Ike Clanton, don't they?'

'That's right. They killed Morgan.'

McMasters nodded his understanding.

'We need a place to use as a temporary headquarters,' Wyatt went on. 'A base of operations, so to speak. We were hoping you could put us up for a while. We can use our own bedrolls, and we'll pay for what food we eat.'

McMasters held a hand up. 'Don't say another word. It would be my pleasure to accommodate you. I hate Ike and the gunmen he's hired out there.'

'We appreciate this,' Doc told him.

'I don't think he knows we're here,' Wyatt continued.

'But of course there's danger to you in this. I wouldn't ask if we had another option.'

'Please, Wyatt. You're the only good thing that's happened to Tombstone in recent memory. But Ike's formed a small army out there on his ranch. I thought you and Virgil were lucky to get out of here alive. Frankly, I'm kind of sorry to see you back. When Ike gets wind of this, he'll send a whirlwind against you.'

'I know. But we won't be here by then. All I want is to gather some provisions and ammunition, and then we'll be on the move. It will be like guerrilla warfare. When we've taken Spence and Charlie down, we'll be gone.'

'Does Ike know you're still in the Territory?'

'Oh, yes,' James said. 'He ambushed us at Contention. He knows we didn't get on the train to California.'

'Behan will have a posse out for us,' Warren put in.

McMasters looked over at his innocent, young face. McMasters was a lean, tough-looking man who was hardened by his outside life. He wore an Ivers & Johnson revolver on his hip, and there were several shotguns and rifles standing around the big room. In a far corner was a stack of beaver and ermine hides, and there was a double bunk on a back wall.

'I see you have your own posse,' McMasters said to Wyatt. 'Look. You don't have enough manpower, Wyatt. I've been looking for an opportunity to make a stand against the Clantons for some time now. I'd like to join up with you.'

Wyatt's eyes narrowed down. 'That's a real nice offer, Sherman. But this is really our fight. It was our brother who was killed.'

'It wasn't Doc's brother,' McMasters responded.

'I felt like a brother to him,' Doc said.

'I have a payback coming, too,' McMasters went on. 'You remember, Wyatt? For my cousin?'

'We need him, Wyatt,' James said.

Wyatt glanced at him, then met McMasters' gaze again. 'Sure, Sherman. We'd be pleased to have you.'

'There's also a friend of mine. A boy named John Johnson. He just arrived in Tombstone. He wore a badge in Wichita for a while. He's good with a gun, Wyatt. Not like you, or even Virgil, but he's already taken a dislike to Ike, and John Ringo. I think he'd like to be a part of this.'

'Can he be trusted to keep his mouth shut and do what he's told?' Doc bluntly asked him.

'I'd trust him with my life,' McMasters said. 'And he'll stand up against a posse, Wyatt. Ike doesn't scare him at all.'

Wyatt hesitated only briefly. 'All right. When you go into town for our provisions, invite him out here. We may need every gun we can scrape together.'

'I'll do that,' McMasters grinned.

Warren was smiling. 'I'm beginning to feel a lot better about all this,' he announced. 'Say, is there someplace out back where I can practice with this revolver James gave me?' James had dug an old Colt out of his saddlebag and given it to Warren to use.

'You can't go out there firing off that piece anywhere near the cabin!' James responded quickly. 'Use your head, Warren!'

Warren looked chagrined. 'I just want to be a help,' he muttered.

'It's all right, Warren,' Wyatt told him. 'I saw you shoot. You'll do just fine.' He turned to Doc. 'All of Behan's posse will be composed of Ike's gunmen, and my guess is that the two we want will be on that posse. Spence and

Charlie. It won't be long now till they'll be out scouring the countryside for us. When we run onto them, or they run onto us, that should end all this, one way or the other.'

'I'm looking forward to it,' McMasters said. 'Look, you boys must be hungry. I'll fix us up some bacon and eggs, and then you all can rest up while I ride into town for supplies.'

'I could use a decent meal,' Doc said, and coughed into a handkerchief.

'I'll help you with that cooking,' Warren said.

McMasters took his old wagon into town that afternoon, and was gone for over two hours. When he returned with provisions and boxes of ammo for their guns, he had John Johnson with him. After they unloaded the wagon, there was time to introduce Johnson to them.

'John, this is Wyatt Earp. You probably know the name,' McMasters suggested. They were all standing around the big table in the cabin.

'Yes, I been reading about you ever since you cleaned up Dodge City,' Johnson grinned. He was tall and lean, with a long nose and bony cheeks. He wore a wide-brim Stetson and silver Mexican spurs on his boots. Over his blue shirt and yellow neckerchief he had donned a sheepskin jacket.

Wyatt nodded to him. 'I heard you did the same thing in Wichita.'

'Oh, that was nothing. We never had any big trouble there. I almost rode down to join you in Dodge.'

Wyatt grinned. 'I could have used you. This here is Doc Holliday, John.'

Johnson's face changed, the grin gone. 'Doc Holliday. I always wanted to meet you, Doc. You're practically a legend in Kansas City.'

Doc grunted. 'I heard they put me in one of those dime novels. They like to make me out a ruthless killer.'

McMasters laughed. 'Are you a ruthless killer, Doc?'

Doc replied with a sober face. 'If the situation demands it.'

That remark elicited a moment of silence, then Wyatt continued, introducing his brothers. Then Wyatt sat on the edge of the table. 'Are you sure you want to be in on this, John? This is personal with all of us here.'

Johnson nodded. 'I understand. But I reckon it's personal with me, too. John Ringo shot and killed a good friend of mine back in Kansas. And just since I arrived here, him and Ike and a couple of other guns of Ike hoorawed me in the Alhambra. Called me out. It would have been four to one, so I backed off. I don't like backing off.'

Wyatt gave him a small grin. 'None of us here does, John. Well, if you're settled on it, we'll be glad to have you. Somewhere along the line, we'll meet up with Behan's posse. Then we'll match posse with posse, and may the best men win.'

Johnson nodded. 'About that posse.'

'Yes?' Doc said.

'I been drinking a little with the editor of the *Epitaph*.' He was referring to the newspaper in Tombstone that had always been fair to the Earps in its reporting.

'He's a good man,' Wyatt said. 'The *Nugget* always reported favorably for the Clantons.'

'He got an interview with Sheriff Behan yesterday. You're right, he's talking revenge for Stilwell's killing. I hear Stilwell was with some men who ambushed you down at Contention.'

'That's right,' Warren interposed. James gave him a look.

'Well, Behan has already formed a posse. Ike volunteered several of his people.'

Wyatt gave Doc a knowing look. 'Do you know whether Pete Spence is on it? And Indian Charlie?'

'Spence will be on it. But right now he's in jail. The townsfolk was in such an uproar about your brother Morgan's killing, they forced Behan to arrest him. But Behan assured the *Epitaph* editor that he'll be released pronto, to ride with the posse.'

'Behan is just going through the motions for the voters,' Wyatt said quietly. 'He wouldn't ever allow a Clanton man to go to prison.'

'Well, he's in the local lock-up till Ike makes bail for him,' Johnson said. 'Ike also supplied John Ringo for the posse, and Phin Clanton, Hank Swilling, and Curly Bill Brocius.'

Doc shook his head. 'What a surprise,' he said sourly.

'But no Indian Charlie?' Wyatt said.

'Oh, that's right. Charlie was mentioned, too. But he's going to join the posse when Spence is released. Behan mentioned Charlie is still hiding out in the hills east of here, in a hunter's cabin, with a couple of friends. He's been scared to death you'd be coming after him. He won't come in till Behan is ready to ride.'

'He's smarter than most of those people Ike hired,' Doc commented. 'And he's not too stupid-proud to run when the occasion requires it.'

Everybody looked over at Wyatt, who was thinking all that over. Both of the men he was after were temporarily isolated from Ike's and Behan's army of guns. That was even better than facing a posse to get at them.

'I wonder how much time we have before Spence is released on bail?' Wyatt said, staring at the floor.

'I got the idea it would be a few days,' Johnson said. 'Ike is off somewhere for a bit, maybe at the McLaury ranch. I'd guess somebody will ride out to get Charlie as soon as that happens. Then they'll be out looking for you.'

'I might know that cabin where Charlie is holed up,' McMasters said. 'There's only one abandoned hunting cabin east of here in the foothills, at least it's the only one I've ever heard of or seen. Used to belong to a prospector, and then a trapper took it over for a while. It's only an hour's ride from here, and I could find it pretty easy. I'd bet money that's where Charlie is.'

'You said he's with a couple of friends?' James asked Johnson.

'That's the way I got it. But listen, my information could be all wrong.'

'Your information is right,' Wyatt said. As the others watched, he dumped a box of .45 cartridges onto the table and began refilling his gunbelt. 'We have to ride out there. It's my best chance at Charlie.'

'When?' Warren asked.

'Now,' Wyatt said. 'As soon as we get saddled up. But you're not going. You and James are staying here to guard the cabin. We have a lot of important stuff here.'

'The hell we are!' James exclaimed. 'I came with you to fight, not nursemaid some damned provisions!'

'That's right!' Warren spoke up belligerently.

Wyatt sighed. 'Look. Charlie isn't surrounded by an army out there. That's why I'm going. Somebody has to stay here, and you two are the most likely candidates. Sherman here and John have more experience at this sort of thing. And you'll have plenty of action later, when we meet Behan's posse.'

'Damn it, Wyatt!' James growled, rubbing his shot arm.

'This is where you're most important to me,' Wyatt said. 'And I don't want an argument every time I make a decision that affects the group.'

The brothers eventually cooled down. 'All right, Wyatt,' Warren conceded.

Wyatt picked up a half-inch thick almanac from the table, one that he had been perusing earlier. 'Mind if I borrow this for a while, Sherman? It has a table of roads at the back that might help us get around in the next few days, if we move around a lot.'

'Sure. Take it with us,' McMasters said.

Wyatt stuffed it into a breast pocket of his shirt, under his dark vest. 'Let's go,' he said.

A half-hour later the four of them rode out toward the hills in the distant east.

The day had warmed up. Johnson had removed the sheepskin, and Wyatt had discarded his long riding-coat, as had Doc. They rode in complete silence, with McMasters leading the way. They were soon in low hills that led into a broad range of mountains at the eastern edge of Cochise County. After they had gotten well into rocky terrain that was all uphill, McMasters stopped and then headed off to the south-east. 'It's not far from here,' he told them.

They rode into scrub pine, where big boulders littered the landscape. Eventually they emerged into a wide clearing backed by tall pines, with a small cabin sitting just in front of them. Just visible, at the rear, three horses were picketed to stakes in the ground.

'That's it,' McMasters said. 'And it's occupied.'

'I see the Indian's mount back there,' Doc said.

'And two others,' Wyatt added. 'I think I've seen Billy Miller on that sorrel.'

'The third man is probably one of Ike's hands too,' Doc surmised.

'They probably haven't seen us yet,' Wyatt said. 'Let's dismount in those trees over there.'

They walked the horses into a small stand of pines, and tethered them there. After they were all dismounted, Wyatt turned to the others.

'I only want Charlie. But they'll all fight when it comes to it.' He drew his right-hand Peacemaker and checked its ammunition, then slid it back into its holster in a fluid motion. 'We won't be taking any prisoners, boys.'

They all stared at him. Doc had a slight grin on his sallow face.

'Do you mean, even if somebody surrenders?' McMasters said.

'I mean, there will be no prisoners,' Wyatt said carefully. 'I don't want Ike to know we were here. What happens here today stays here. Do we all understand each other?'

McMasters and Johnson exchanged a sober look. 'We understand, Wyatt.'

'Sherman, you're good with horses. Make a wide circuit around the cabin to the east, and make your way to their mounts. Calm them down so they don't make a fuss. We'll need the element of surprise.'

McMasters nodded. 'I can do that.'

'John, I want you to move over to the south and situate yourself beside that big boulder. Get that Winchester out of your carbine boot and make sure it's loaded. If anybody gets past us, cut him down. Sherman will take care of anyone that makes it to the horses.'

'You don't want us to go in with you?' Johnson said with surprise. 'There are at least three of them in there.'

'Doc and I have handled those odds before,' Wyatt said. 'Any questions?'

'You're taking a lot on your own shoulders,' McMasters commented.

'That's where it ought to be,' Wyatt told him. 'Don't worry, Sherman. You may get into it, anyway. And there's nothing more important in this than keeping their horses quiet. OK. You and John can take up your positions.'

Doc and Wyatt remained in the cover of the trees as the other two men headed off in different directions. Soon Johnson was waving at them from the protective boulder a hundred yards away, and then they saw McMasters emerge from the trees behind the horses. Charlie's horse guffered as he approached them, but then it and the others accepted him. He stepped out and gave Wyatt a thumbs-up.

Doc and Wyatt removed their spurs from their riding-boots, and Doc slid his revolvers in and out of their holsters a couple times. Then they headed up a slight incline toward the cabin.

There was no window on the front of the cabin, so they were hidden from any view inside, so long as the door was closed. They approached slowly and silently. At last they were at the door.

Wyatt put his ear to the door, and heard Billy Miller talking inside. Miller was one of Ike's part-time hirelings.

'Yeah, Ike will be sending somebody out here for us any minute now. I can't wait to join up with that posse. I just hope I'm the first man to get a shot at that coward Earp.'

'So you think Wyatt is some kind of *cobarde*?' The voice of Indian Charlie came to him.

'They say he shot Frank Stilwell down in cold blood,' Miller responded.

He had ridden out to the cabin to advise Charlie what had happened at Contention, and to prepare him to return to join Behan's posse shortly.

'He didn't give Stilwell a chance,' a third voice said, one unfamiliar to Wyatt. He must have joined Charlie earlier, as a bodyguard.

'That's Ike's version,' Charlie said. 'I think that bastard is coming after me, though. I feel his presence, *amigos.*'

'Naw, he's way down near the border by now. Figuring he's damn lucky to be alive.'

Wyatt stepped back from the door, and nodded to Doc. Then he aimed a kick at the door latch and busted the door inward.

There was a loud crashing sound as the door almost came off its hinges, and Wyatt and Doc stepped through it, guns drawn. Charlie was seated at a table, and Miller and a third ranch man stood nearby. While Wyatt's and Doc's eyes adjusted to the darker light, Miller and the third man drew their guns and began firing at the same moment as their adversaries.

The resulting chaos was ear-splitting. No word was spoken by either side. There was no time for words, or warnings. There was only one moment in eternity to try to salvage mortality. Guns roared and roared again, the noise caroming off the close walls and doubling its intensity. Hot lead flew in all directions, with small suns erupting from gunbarrels for a split second and then dying in the wake of reverberation. Miller's first shot hit the door behind Wyatt and the second one, after he had been slugged by Wyatt's first shot, tore at Wyatt's collar but missed flesh. The third man got off one shot at Doc, narrowly missing his head by a half-inch, before Doc put two slugs in him, one in the side and the second one exploding his heart like a paper bag. Wyatt had fired twice, hitting Miller in the middle chest and left eye. Charlie had gotten to his feet at last, and got a round off at Wyatt, his face now frozen with terror. His shot burned a mark along Wyatt's left forearm but didn't break the flesh. Wyatt's third shot was purposely high, clubbing Charlie in the left shoulder.

Billy Miller's good eye had saucered as he raced backwards, slamming against the rear wall and leaving a crimson stain there as he slid to the floor. The other ranch hand had grabbed the table as he fell and took it down with him. Charlie hit the floor hard on his back, groaning now in pain.

The gunsmoke was so thick Wyatt could taste it. Doc walked over to Miller and the third man, and nodded. 'They punched their last dogie.' He grinned.

Wyatt walked over to Charlie, figuring he was out of the fight. But Charlie's right hand, hidden behind the overturned table, suddenly had his Starr Army .44 back in it. Weakly he fired once before Wyatt could react. The banging shot hit Wyatt in the chest, and punched him backwards, where he fell against the doorjamb. He hung there for a moment while Doc stared in disbelief.

'Wyatt!'

Charlie couldn't believe his good luck. He squeezed the trigger again, but there was only a dull clicking sound.

Wyatt felt his chest, and pushed off the wall. He reached into his shirt, and pulled out the thick little almanac he had taken from McMasters' cabin. The bullet had passed all the way through it, and its nose protruded from the inner surface. It had bruised Wyatt, but not killed him.

Without waiting to see the extent of Wyatt's wound, Doc turned savagely on Charlie, and aimed his Peacemaker at Charlie's head. 'You damn snake in the grass! Take this to half-breed hell with you!'

'Hold it, Doc,' Wyatt called to him.

Doc turned again.

'I'm all right. The book saved me.' He massaged his chest as he walked over to Charlie, still on the floor.

'I had to try,' Charlie told him, gasping it out. He was a bulky man, with reddish skin and a hooked nose. He wore a pigtail under a bowler hat, which now lay on the floor. 'You're Wyatt Earp.'

Wyatt holstered his revolvers. Charlie still held his Starr in his hand. 'Reload that piece, and holster it,' Wyatt told him.

Charlie shrugged, and obeyed.

'Now get on your feet.'

'My shoulder. I think you broke it.'

'I said, get on your feet.'

'Let me put one in him right now,' Doc said.

Charlie slowly got to his feet, using the fallen table. He drunkenly faced Wyatt, as McMasters appeared in the doorway, with Johnson just behind him.

'I knew you was coming for me,' Charlie said. 'I see things like that.'

'I want you to admit you killed Morgan,' Wyatt said in a low, hard voice. His chest was beginning to throb pain. 'You and Stilwell and Pete Spence.'

Charlie shrugged again. 'Why not? Sure, we did it.'

'Why would you back-shoot a man who had never done you any harm?' Wyatt growled at him.

'You boys was ruining everything for us,' Charlie said. 'We knew we had to get rid of you, so things would be good again. It was just business, Wyatt.'

'You rattlesnake!' Doc grated out.

Charlie glanced at the two newcomers. 'Well? Which one of you wants to do it? It's a good day to die.'

'Which way is Behan's posse going to ride?' Wyatt went on.

'I don't know. But I guess he'll head out south toward Contention. That's where you was last seen. Listen. I'll go over to your side. I can run circles around any posse of Behan's. Take me in, Wyatt. What's past is past.'

'What's past will always be with us,' Wyatt said soberly. 'Fill your hand with iron, Charlie. If you kill me, these boys will leave you to yourself. I promise it.'

Charlie raised himself up a bit, and studied the faces of the other three. 'I can't beat you, Wyatt. Nobody can.'

'It's different, I'm hurt. And it's your only chance. Draw, Charlie.'

Suddenly Charlie looked desperate. Suddenly he wanted to live. If there was just a chance in a hundred, he had to take it.

He pushed the overturned table away from him, and assumed a fighting stance. His right hand went over his holster. His eyes looked wild.

'I'll expect you boys to get me a doc for this shoulder,' he said despairingly. 'And I'll demand a big bonus from Ike, when I get back to the ranch.'

Then he went for his gun.

Actually, Charlie was pretty fast, even with his shot shoulder. But by the time he had cleared leather Wyatt's Peacemakers had both fired twice, riddling Charlie's chest with lead.

Charlie's gun went off then, splintering wood in the floor while he jumped backwards as if jerked on a wire, and hit the floor behind him hard. When Wyatt went and stood over him, he was already dead.

'Good riddance,' Doc commented acidly behind him.

'Two down,' Wyatt said in a tight voice. 'One to go.'

'Let's get out of here,' McMasters suggested. 'We have some hard riding ahead of us.'

CHAPTER SEVEN

It was almost dark when they arrived back at McMasters' cabin.

Johnson wanted to bring the dead men's horses and saddles back with them, and McMasters wanted to bury the corpses, but neither of those things happened. Wyatt knew they couldn't sell the horses in Tombstone without risk of discovery. He set the animals loose, leaving the saddlery behind the cabin. Doc said pugnaciously that he would shoot anybody in the leg who tried to put 'those three scorpions' underground, and McMasters gave up on the idea.

Inside the cabin at last, with their mounts unsaddled and fed, McMasters and Johnson relieved themselves of their gunbelts before they started on the evening meal, but Wyatt and Doc kept theirs on, as they usually did under circumstances like these.

'Well?' James eventually said to Wyatt. 'What happened out there? Was Charlie there?' He and Warren were frying up some salted beef, and boiling potatoes in a big, black pot.

'Charlie is with his ancestors,' Doc answered for Wyatt. 'And he took two of his snake pals along with him for company.'

'Billy Miller and another of Ike's ranch hands,' McMasters reported.

'Damn,' Warren muttered, looking up from the potato pot.

A short time later they were all sitting around McMasters' big round dining table, wolfing down the meat and potatoes. Wyatt ate ravenously, finding he had an enormous appetite. He hadn't said a half-dozen words since their return. Now he looked over at James. 'Anybody come past here today?'

James shook his head. 'No, it was real quiet. You should have taken us.'

Wyatt gave him an acid look. 'Just think you're in the US Cavalry, boys. Where everybody is assigned a specific task. And performs it without question.'

James looked down at his meal. 'We're not in the army, Wyatt.'

Wyatt stopped eating. 'From now on you're in a war. Remember that. Think like a soldier, James. From now on you don't have the luxury of independent thinking. You'll do what's best for this little platoon. Period.'

'We can do that, Wyatt,' Warren spoke up. There was a silence around the table, then he changed the subject. 'I'm glad you got Charlie. That leaves just Pete Spence, right?'

'That's right,' Doc intervened, glancing at Wyatt's solemn face.

Wyatt looked up at the group. 'If Ike comes after us in person, I want him, too, of course. But I won't follow him back to his little army to get him. That would make it too easy for him. We have to find him out in the open, in Behan's posse. If the opportunity presents itself in that situation, I'll kill him, too.'

Another silence, as they ate quietly.

At last Doc spoke. 'If that sonofabitch don't go to hell, there's no point in having one.'

'I'll second that,' Johnson said.

McMasters looked over at Wyatt. 'You want to wait till Spence rides out as part of the posse, or go after him in Tombstone?'

Wyatt was finished eating. He raised a cup of coffee to his lips and sipped slowly at it, thinking. 'It would be quite an operation, to go after him while he's being held in jail. It might be better to confront Behan's posse later.'

'It's about six of one to half a dozen of the other,' Doc put in. 'If you get to him in the jail, it's over. And there's something else. Ike might be back from his visit to the McLaurys, and could be staying at the Grand Hotel where he keeps a suite of rooms. You'd never have a better opportunity.'

Wyatt glanced up at him. 'You worry my blood like a woman, Doc.' He gave a small grin. When they had first come in McMasters had gotten a soft bandage for Wyatt's chest, where a big, red welt and a three-inch-wide bruise gave him pain like a toothache. But he paid no attention to it. 'And of course they wouldn't be expecting us.'

'They don't know me well there,' Johnson said. 'I could go down to the jail first and scout out who's there on duty.'

'I could go with him,' Warren offered. 'Nobody there has ever set eyes on me.'

Wyatt sighed, and nodded. 'Yes, Warren. You could.'

Both Warren and James were surprised at that.

'Well, what would I do?' James said rather loudly.

Wyatt met his brother's anxious look. 'We'll all go in.'

James' face brightened. 'Now you're talking!'

'I heard one of Ike's men has been given the temporary

position of town marshal, just to handle this situation,' Johnson recalled. 'To watch over Spence and make sure there's no trouble from local citizens. Seems like the name was Barnes.'

'That would be Johnny Barnes,' James said. 'He used to come into the Oriental a lot. Swaggers around like a real gunman. If he's alone, he wouldn't give us much trouble.'

'The problem is,' McMasters said, 'we don't even know he's still there.'

Everybody looked at him.

'That thought hadn't escaped me,' Wyatt said. He was bare-headed, and his thick, dark hair was still slightly mussed from the encounter earlier. He ran a slender finger through his handlebar mustache, pensively. 'I realize it's all a big risk, on several levels. But the idea of possibly ending all this now has gotten into my head and I can't shake it. I'm going in.'

'Good,' James said quickly.

'I'm with Wyatt,' Doc said. 'If we can drop that jackal while he's right here, instead of riding all over the countryside trying to find him, I'm all for it. When do you want to do it, Wyatt?'

Wyatt thought for a moment. 'I don't think we have any choice,' he said to them. 'We have to go tonight.'

Everybody but Doc eyed him with surprise.

'What?' McMasters said. 'We just rode all day to get Indian Charlie! We need rest, Wyatt!'

'We won't leave till midnight. We can all get some sleep till then. Time is not our friend right now, Sherman. Every hour we spend here is risky. For all of us. Of course, if you don't want to go, I'll understand.'

McMasters sighed. 'If you go, I go,' he said.

'My God. Tonight,' Warren mumbled.

'You wanted action, kid,' Wyatt told him. 'Now you might just get it.'

Warren bolstered himself. 'I'm up for it, brother,' he said.

Doc rose from the table. 'Excuse me, gentlemen,' he said. 'These old bones need a lie-down. I'm hitting the sack.' He had been given the extra bunk, as the one most needy.

Warren rose, an excited flush on his young face. 'I'll clear these dishes up real fast. We have a big night ahead of us.'

'Not tonight, Warren,' Doc grunted. 'There will be plenty of time tomorrow. If there is a tomorrow. If not, let someone else do it.'

With that he climbed up onto his cot and fell directly to sleep.

There was no moon that night. They were all up and had the horses saddled by 11.30 on Doc's railroad watch. They left the cabin in single file under a pitch-black sky, with Wyatt in the lead.

It was less than twenty miles into town, but it was about a two-hour ride. When they arrived on the outskirts of town it was almost two o'clock. The streets were dark and empty. The six of them reined in near the hostelry, which was closed for the night. Wyatt looked down the dark street. Down past the Oriental saloon, and the Alhambra, and the two hotels and Camillus Fly's rooming-house.

He had been gone less than a week, and it seemed like a year to him. In his mind's eye he saw the town as it had been before the trouble. James serving drinks at the Oriental, joking with the patrons. A dance hall that usually rang with music and laughter. When they passed under the balconies of the Cosmopolitan Hotel, where the brothers had kept apartments on a monthly basis, Wyatt remembered all the pleasant evenings there, with the women serving them some Spanish dish like paella, and Morgan complaining it was too hot for his taste, and hefty Virgil letting his belt out a notch.

He let a long breath out. 'Warren, I'm stationing you here. If anybody approaches town from this direction, take your hat off and wave it toward the jail. Sherman will be watching from outside on the street. James, I'll put you in a similar spot on the other end of town. Ike might be sending patrols out. In case we show up.'

'OK, Wyatt,' Warren said.

James nodded moodily. It seemed as though he would never see any real action.

'Doc, John and I will go in. Barnes might have company there.'

'What happens if somebody does show up?' James wondered.

'After you've signaled, you join us here. Are we all set on this?'

'Let's do it,' Johnson said.

They left Warren there, and rode on down to the jail. They passed Bob Hatch's poolroom, and Wyatt remembered the small confrontation there with Pony Deal, John Ringo and Curly Bill Brocius, three of Ike's most deadly gunmen. Ringo, Deal and Barnes would reportedly be on the posse that came after him.

A moment later they reined up before the marshal's office and jail. They were two-thirds of the way along the length of Allen Street. Wyatt motioned to James. James nodded, and slowly walked his mount on down the street, to its end. When he got there, he and Warren were just visible in the darkness.

The other four dismounted and wrapped their reins over a long hitching rail. 'Watch both ends of town,' Wyatt told McMasters. 'We're going in.' He looked through a small window but couldn't see anything in there.

'Be careful, Wyatt,' McMasters told him.

Wyatt entered first, his guns still holstered. Doc and Johnson came close behind, fanning out onto either side of the door. There was the desk where Virgil and Wyatt used to sit and do paperwork. There was a billboard on one wall, and there was still a Wanted dodger there that Wyatt had tacked up himself. There was nobody in the room.

'Where the hell is he?' Johnson grunted out, his lean face taut.

Just at that moment, Johnny Barnes came striding down a short corridor to the rear of the building, where there were two holding cells. He looked up at the last minute before entering the room, and the first thing he saw was Wyatt. He stopped dead in his tracks, and his hand went automatically to his gun.

'I wouldn't do that,' Wyatt said easily. 'Not if you want to live through the night, cowboy.'

Barnes let his hand drop slowly to his side. Eyes big.

'Come on in here,' Wyatt told him.

Barnes moved cautiously into the office. 'Don't kill me, Wyatt.'

'Just keep your hand away from that six-shooter,' Doc advised him.

Barnes nodded nervously. 'Doc. Look, they pinned this badge on me, Wyatt. I didn't want it. You can have it back.'

'Forget the badge,' Wyatt growled at him. 'Is Pete Spence back there?'

'Oh, he's gone,' Barnes said, his mouth as dry as old paper. 'Ike made bail for him this afternoon.'

Wyatt frowned at him. 'You wouldn't want to be lying to us, Barnes?'

'No, no, I wouldn't!' Barnes choked out. He was a rather short fellow, with a round, pockmarked face. He was wearing dungarees and stovepipe boots, and had flaming red hair. 'You can check for yourself.'

'We will,' Wyatt told him. 'John, take a look back there.'

Johnson nodded, and walked down the short corridor to the rear, drawing his revolver.

'Is there anybody else watching the jail?' Wyatt pursued.

'No, it's just me,' Barnes said.

Johnson returned from his inspection. 'There's nobody back there,' he reported.

Wyatt let out a long breath. All this risk had been for nothing. He walked over to the poster-board and swung his fist hard against it. Both Barnes and Johnson jumped slightly, and Barnes began breathing hard.

'Damn it,' Wyatt grated out. He turned and burned a fiery look onto Barnes. 'He'll be part of Behan's posse, won't he?'

Barnes hesitated.

'Now isn't the time to start lying, cowpoke,' Doc suggested.

Barnes was very tight. He licked dry lips, and met Wyatt's stony gaze. 'I expect so,' he said in a half-whisper.

'Who else will be riding out after us?'

'I'm not really sure.'

'Spit it out, damn you!' Wyatt barked at him.

Barnes swallowed hard. 'Well, there would be Behan and Ike, of course,' he said nervously.'And I think Ringo will go, and Curly Bill, Phin Clanton, Pony Deal. Oh, yeah.

Billy Miller and Indian Charlie.'

Johnson shot a tight grin at Doc. Doc returned it, and turned to Barnes. 'And you, too. Right, Johnny?'

Barnes looked like he might faint away. 'Hell, no! Not me, Doc! Ike wants me right here!'

'He's lying through his teeth,' Doc said. He drew a revolver casually. 'Pick out a nice spot for me in hell, you mangy dog.'

'Wait, Doc,' Wyatt said heavily. 'He's been co-operating.'

Doc turned angrily to him. 'Wait for what? This lowlife is going to be out there beating the bushes to kill you! You want to wait for him to put a bullet in your brain from behind a rock somewhere?'

'Doc's right, Wyatt,' Johnson said.

Wyatt was frustrated and short-tempered. 'Who the hell is running this show? You, Doc? Or maybe you want the job, John?' Fiercely.

'No, of course not,' Johnson said quietly.

Barnes was still standing there breathless, sweat trickling down his sides from under his arms, watching Doc's still unholstered Peacemaker. Doc and Wyatt exchanged a long, brittle look. After a moment, Doc reholstered his weapon.

'You need a keeper, damn you!' Doc said in a sibilant voice. 'I'll be outside.'

He turned and left, leaving Wyatt and Johnson with Barnes. Wyatt turned to the broad-shouldered ranch hand.

'I just saved your life, Barnes.'

'I know.'

'If I see you out there in Behan's posse, you're a dead man.'

'I won't be there,' Barnes promised. 'You can take that

116

to the bank.'

Wyatt shook his head slowly. 'You're not up to this, Barnes. You ought to go get yourself legitimate work somewhere. You might live longer.'

'I'll think on that,' Barnes told him.

When they were outside again, Doc had already advised McMasters of Pete Spence's escape from their net, and James had been waved back. As they went to the hitching rail, Johnson turned to Wyatt.

'I think Doc's right. He'll be in their posse.' He spoke very carefully.

'I know I'm right,' Doc said morosely. 'I hope you don't live to regret it, Wyatt.' His voice was softer now. Friendlier.

Wyatt looked over at his old friend. 'We can't kill every Clanton hand who might take a shot at us later, Doc. But we're not finished here tonight.'

James had just ridden up, and Johnson reported to him. Warren was still down at the far end of the street, where they had come in.

'What do you mean, we're not finished?' James asked.

'Has anybody taken a look at the Grand Hotel since we've been inside? There's lights on in the Clanton suite now.'

Everybody stared down the street toward the hotel.

'Well, what do you know!' Doc said, his lean face brightening.

'Have you heard anybody come up on the back side of the hotel, Sherman?' Wyatt asked him.

'No, nothing,' McMasters said.

'Well, there's somebody up there,' Wyatt said. 'Maybe got up for a drink. Or we might have woke them. I don't see anybody in the windows.'

'You're right, we have to check this out,' Doc said. 'Ike could be up there. Or Pete Spence, or both of them.'

'Ike could be staying in town to get the posse together tomorrow morning,' James added.

Wyatt nodded. Suddenly the frustration evaporated. 'It would be perfect. The general cut off from his army. Well, let's find out. Sherman, you stay outside again. James, you and John join Warren. Doc and I will handle this.'

James was through arguing with him. He and Johnson saddled up and walked their mounts quietly down the street. Wyatt, Doc and McMasters led their animals to the hotel hitch.

'If you hear gunfire in there, and we don't come back out,' Wyatt told McMasters, 'get on your horse and join the others, and ride out. My brothers won't want to go. You'll have to persuade them.'

McMasters let out a long breath. 'Right.'

Wyatt and Doc climbed the steps to the hotel entrance, and looked in through the glass in the door. The night clerk was nowhere to be seen. Wyatt opened the door and they entered.

'He's probably in the office sleeping,' Wyatt said.

They started for the stair, as the Clanton suite was on the second floor.

But then a sleepy-looking, bespectacled clerk came through a door from a private office. When he saw them, his eyes widened.

'Marshal Earp! Doc Holliday! Good God, what are you doing back in Tombstone?'

Wyatt walked over to the short counter between him and the clerk. The fellow was small and plump, with pink cheeks and balding hair.

'Who's upstairs in the Clanton rooms?'

The clerk tried to speak, but his tongue stuck to the roof of his mouth. He tried again. 'I don't rightly know. Somebody come in earlier, I guess. When the day clerk was on. I'd tell you if I knew.' His tongue was clicking on his mouth.

'He's telling the truth,' Doc said.

Wyatt caught the fellow's eyes. 'Listen carefully to me. We're going upstairs to have a little talk with whoever's there. If you make any noise down here, or go for Sheriff Behan, I'll kill you on the way out of town.'

The clerk was gently trembling now. 'Yes, Marshal.'

'And if Barnes comes in here, you tell him he'd be safer not coming upstairs. You got it?'

'I'll do that.' Tightly.

Wyatt and Doc then continued to the stairway, where they climbed up to the second floor. The Clanton suite took up most of the front of the hotel at that level. In a moment they stood before its door. Light came through the crack at the bottom, but they could hear no sound from within.

'How do you want to do it?' Doc said.

'Let's show them we're civilized men,' Wyatt said, with a half-grin.

He reached forward and knocked on the door. Neither man drew his gun.

There was a brief delay, then there was a voice on the other side.

'Who is it?'

'Open it up and find out,' Wyatt called through the door.

Another delay, then the door was unlocked from inside. Slowly it opened a mere crack. Wyatt could see part of the face of Hank Swilling, one of Ike's top guns, and a fellow

119

who used the suite regularly. The man's face registered shock.

'Damn!' He tried to reclose the door, but Wyatt had wedged his foot in the opening. Now he shoved hard on it, knocking Swilling backward a few steps. In the next moment, he and Doc were inside. Swilling was dressed and armed, but nobody drew a weapon.

Wyatt looked around the room. It was a parlor, with two big sofas and several overstuffed chairs. A card-table stood over near a wall, with straight chairs around it. On a table before a sofa sat a bottle of bourbon, half-full. Two unwashed glasses sat beside it.

'Where's Ike?' Wyatt demanded.

'What the hell are you doing here?' the lanky Swilling said. 'Are you crazy, Earp?'

'I asked you a question,' Wyatt said.

'You can't bust in here like you own the place and expect to order anybody around,' Swilling blustered. 'You don't wear a badge no more.'

Wyatt pushed his coat back to reveal a Peacemaker, and when he spoke, it was in a low, quiet voice. 'I'm not playing games here tonight, Swilling. I'm not in the mood. Who's here besides you? And I won't ask again.'

Swilling glanced at the big gun. 'Ike ain't here. Ringo is in the bedroom. Ike sent us into town to keep a lookout for you.'

'Is Ike in town?'

'He's out at the ranch. He'll be in tomorrow with some men for Behan's posse. You better not be here.'

'You keep on with that mouth, I'll put a chunk of lead in your liver,' Doc growled at him.

Swilling glanced toward Doc. 'I'm just telling you like it is, boys. The whole damn countryside will be swarming with armed men tomorrow. All looking to collect a reward on your scalps.' A slow grin.

Wyatt shook his head. 'Where's Pete Spence?'

'He was in town earlier. When Ike bailed him out of jail. But tonight he's out at the ranch with Ike and the rest.'

Just then John Ringo appeared in a doorway to a bedroom. He was armed, like Swilling, and as he focused on Wyatt and Doc, a heavy scowl grew on his square face. 'Well, look at this. I wish Ike was here to see this. You two come back to turn yourselves in?'

'They're looking for Pete Spence,' Swilling put in quickly, seeing the look in Ringo's eyes.

Wyatt saw the look, too. Ringo hadn't forgotten his embarrassment by Wyatt at the pool hall, before the Earps left town. 'Haven't seen you for a while, John. I thought maybe you'd rode out.'

Ringo took that as an insult on top of humiliation. 'Run from you, you fancy-pants dandy?' he said, in a breathless tone.

Swilling looked more nervous. 'Take it easy, John.'

'I've had enough boning from this tin-badge strutter. I'll bet he ain't half as good as his swelled head tells him.'

Doc laughed in his throat at that, and then coughed fitfully for a moment. 'No, he isn't half as good. He's better than he knows.'

Ringo turned a blistering look on Doc. 'You're lucky Ike ain't here, you tooth-puller. Neither one of you would leave this room alive!'

'If Ike was here, he'd be lying dead now,' Doc said pleasantly.

'Maybe you boys better leave,' Swilling suggested hopefully. 'We'll tell Ike you was here. I reckon he'll want to return the visit.'

Wyatt smiled. 'We'll be leaving town shortly. I recommend you two do the same. Mexico might be a good place to hide.'

Ringo's eyes suddenly burned with hot fire. 'Run to Mexico? How about this instead, Earp?'

Ringo was one of Ike's fastest guns, and he was very sure of himself. But as his hand went for the gun on his hip, both Wyatt and Doc drew down in lightning-fast motions that Ringo couldn't follow until he saw their guns leveled on his chest. His gun was barely clear of its holster.

Neither Wyatt nor Doc fired, waiting for Ringo's gun to be leveled at one of them. But it wasn't. Seeing he was easily beat, Ringo lost his nerve despite the anger in his gut.

'Don't, Doc,' Wyatt said without looking at him.

Ringo swallowed hard, and returned the pistol to its holster. He looked at the floor now, breathing heavily.

'Hell,' Doc grunted. 'This is getting tiresome, Wyatt.'

They both reholstered their weapons. 'Like I said,' Wyatt remarked then, ignoring Doc, 'better make it Mexico.'

Ringo looked up at him. The hatred was still there, burning inside him, but his fear had smothered it. 'I wish you was in hell with your back broke,' he muttered.

'You ought to be on the floor with your boots pointing at the sky,' Doc growled.

'When Ike catches up to you two,' Ringo said hoarsely, 'he'll stick your heads on trophy poles and parade them around town. Then he'll sell them to a circus, so kids can pay a quarter to come and look at your pickled remains.'

Wyatt shook his head. He and Doc headed for the door, their riding spurs clinking in the new silence. When they got there, Wyatt turned back to the others.

'When you see Pete Spence, boys. . . .'
'Yeah?' Swilling said balefully.
'Tell him he's a walking dead man.'
Then they were gone.

CHAPTER EIGHT

They didn't arrive back at McMasters' cabin until just before dawn. Everybody went directly to bed except Wyatt, who volunteered to stand watch for a while. Actually, he was too energized to sleep. He went out to his horse and slid his American Arms twelve-gauge shotgun with its sawed-off barrel from a saddle scabbard, and brought it inside to clean it. While he worked, he thought of Virgil, hoping he arrived in California without incident, and figuring the family had Morgan buried by now. Morgan's death bothered him more than anything ever had. Morgan had been just a part-time deputy, and didn't really like carrying a gun. Wyatt had been instrumental in getting him into lawing. Morgan helped deal faro bar at the Oriental, and rode shotgun on the stage regularly. If Wyatt hadn't led him into wearing a badge, he might still be alive. And if Wyatt had killed Ike at the OK Corral when he had the chance, Morgan might be alive, too. So Morgan's death stuck in Wyatt's craw, giving him a heavy feeling in his chest that he figured would never go away. The weight had been lightened some when Frank Stilwell and Indian Charlie met their Maker. And it would be lightened further still when Pete Spence answered for his crime. But it would never be gone. Not completely.

Wyatt managed a couple hours of sleep before the others began waking up. McMasters and Warren fixed breakfast for all of them, while John Johnson went out to tend the animals. James couldn't get himself awake, and Doc looked terrible. He had had several coughing fits in the night, and woke up with a bloody handkerchief in hand. His tuberculosis was getting worse. But he never mentioned it, and didn't want others to talk about it.

'Well,' Doc said as they ate their bacon and eggs. 'Behan will be combing the streets of Tombstone for us this morning to make sure we left.'

'They'll go door to door,' McMasters said. 'Till they're satisfied you rode back out.'

'They might harass some of our supporters,' James suggested.

'Ringo and Deal will probably beat on people,' Johnson said.

'Behan will hold them down,' Wyatt told them, sipping at his coffee. 'He has to be re-elected one of these days soon. He can't go too far for Ike.'

'What will they do next?' Warren wondered.

'They'll search all of Cochise County,' Doc said. 'But they won't come clear out here. Sherman here isn't that well-known in town.'

'Warren,' Wyatt said, 'when you finish up there, why don't you ride out west of here a mile and stand watch. I'll send somebody to relieve you later.'

Warren nodded with his mouth full. 'Sure, Wyatt.'

'It would be fine with me if we had it out right here,' Wyatt said thoughtfully. 'If we set up a proper ambush, we could take them.'

'I think they'll head south,' Doc said. 'They probably

think we found us a headquarters down there. They've guessed we're not leaving the territory now.'

Wyatt looked around the table. 'This is going to get serious now, boys. I don't want you or John, Sherman, to be misled. This is going to be a knock-down fight now between us and them, and I intend to take the fight to them. Any man that wants out of this now will be understood. And that includes my two brothers. It's me and Doc they want.'

McMasters shook his head. 'If ever there was a good fight, Wyatt, this is it. I'm in all the way.'

'Same here,' Johnson agreed.

'You don't even have to ask Warren and me,' James said with a frown. 'They wanted a war. Well, now they've got one.'

'That's right!' Warren exclaimed.

Doc grinned at their *naïveté*. 'Behan's posse might be twice as big as our little group here. We're going to have to be smarter than them.'

James was about to reply when they all heard the sound of a horse approaching the cabin from the east, away from town. Wyatt and Doc were both on their feet in an instant, guns drawn. The horse stopped just outside the cabin. Wyatt motioned to McMasters.

'Take a look.'

McMasters went to the door, and opened it, unarmed. A.O. Wallace, the Tombstone justice of the peace, stood there, having just dismounted. Wyatt and Doc exchanged a curious look, and stepped back into shadow.

'Ah, Mr McMasters!' Wallace cried out. He was a big, heavy man with a pot belly and dirty straw hair that stuck out from under a bowler hat. 'I heard you'd taken up this place! How fortunate for me to find you home! May I stop in for a cup of coffee? I've been riding all morning, and it's still two hours to Tombstone. I've just come off my monthly circuit, and am in need of a short rest.'

McMasters hesitated, but Wyatt spoke up from inside. 'Invite him in.'

McMasters understood. To turn him away would create suspicion. 'Yes, please,' McMasters said stiffly. 'I have some coffee boiling.'

When Wallace entered he stopped abruptly just inside the door, and his jaw dropped open. 'Oh, dear!' he gasped out.

'As you see, I have some other visitors,' McMasters said. 'I think you know Wyatt, Doc and James.'

Wallace ran a hand across his mouth. 'Yes, of course.' He had been in the Clanton camp from the beginning. 'Good to see you again, Wyatt. Doc.'

They had reholstered their guns. 'Wallace,' Wyatt greeted him soberly.

McMasters went on: 'And that's a friend of mine from town, John Johnson. John used to wear a badge in Wichita.'

Wallace nodded, still trying to understand what he had walked into. 'Yes, but . . .' he stammered, 'you're supposed to be down at Contention, Wyatt. What brings you up this way again?'

'The murder of my brother brings me here,' Wyatt said in a hard voice.

'Oh, Morgan,' Wallace said, regaining his composure. He removed the bowler and laid it on the table. It was midday, and he had a dew of sweat on his forehead. 'Yes, I don't think I had an opportunity to offer my condolences. A terrible thing, that shooting. Pete Spence has been arrested as a participant, but I'm afraid there's no real evidence to convict. I do hope we find the real culprits, though. Some folks are saying it was out-of-towners. Drifters. We may never know the truth about it.'

'Oh, we know the truth, Wallace,' Doc spat out. 'Three of Ike Clanton's boys did the cowardly deed on Ike's orders.'

Wallace looked shocked. 'Why, that's an awful story!' he exclaimed, taking a kerchief to his brow. 'Ike Clanton order a murder? That just sounds a bit fantastic, Doc! Why, he had a chance to kill you at the corral, Wyatt, and chose to try to disarm you instead!'

'Is that what he told you?' Wyatt growled at him.

'That weasel was afraid to draw on Wyatt,' Doc said. 'That's why he's still alive. Wyatt wouldn't kill a coward with his gun still in its holster.'

'Well,' Wallace stammered. 'All I know is what I heard, of course. That's why there had to be a prosecution, Wyatt. There were all those conflicting stories.'

'The prosecution happened because of Ike's influence on Behan, and Mayor Clum,' James spoke up.

Wallace looked over at him, and was becoming uncomfortable with all of the hostility in the room. 'Look, gentlemen, I'm an impartial observer in this. I'm as hopeful that the real culprits who killed Morgan are caught and brought to justice as any of you.'

'We know who the culprits are,' Doc said in a hard voice. 'Stilwell and Indian Charlie have already paid their debt. Now it's just Pete Spence.'

Wallace hadn't known of the shoot-out at Contention, nor of Charlie's recent demise. Suddenly he looked scared. He licked dry lips. 'You took your badge off, Wyatt. I hope those killings were under the color of the law. And I've already told you. There's no real evidence against Pete.'

'We have our evidence,' Wyatt told him, reseating himself on a chair beside the table. 'Why don't you have that cup of coffee now, Wallace?'

Wallace tried a grin, but it didn't work. 'Oh, yes. I almost forgot. Thank you, I will.'

Warren got him a cup of coffee as he seated himself across the table from Wyatt. Doc sat down, too. Warren and James stood over by the fireplace. McMasters went over to straighten his bunk, and Johnson poured himself another cup of coffee, standing near James and Warren. As Wallace sipped at his coffee, a tight silence settled into the cabin for long moments. At last Wallace spoke again.

'This is very good coffee, Sherman. Do you get it in town?'

McMasters looked up at him somberly, and nodded.

'We can't allow you to just ride out of here now,' Wyatt suddenly said.

Wallace looked over at him as if Wyatt had slapped him in the face. 'What do you mean? I have business in Tombstone, Wyatt. I'm the justice of the peace. I have to make reports on my circuit ride.'

'You'll report our presence here to the Clantons,' Wyatt said, looking down at his coffee cup.

'Why, there's no need for that,' Wallace argued, his face flushed now. He was a rather obese fellow, and fat crowded his eyes and mouth. 'I have my own business to attend to.'

'Maybe the posse will be gone before he gets back,' James suggested to the room.

'Maybe,' Doc said. 'But we can't depend on that.'

'There's a posse?' Wallace said tensely. 'Then I guess Behan has issued warrants for your arrests.'

'Behan may want to arrest us,' Wyatt said. 'But I'm sure Ike has other ideas.'

'Look,' Wallace said quickly. 'If you come in with me, they'll have to go by the book. Arrest you and give you a fair trial.'

'We're not finished yet,' Doc told him menacingly.

Warren looked over at Wyatt. 'That's not a bad offer, is it, Wyatt? They let you off once before. There are people behind you in Tombstone.'

James regarded him as if he had just lost his mind. 'Ike has an army of gunslingers back there, Warren! Just waiting for us to show ourselves, so they can gun us down! And it would all be legal, now that warrants are out on us! Haven't you been listening to anything we've said?'

Warren hung his head. 'It was just an idea. Sorry. I keep forgetting we're not in civilized country.'

Wallace caught Wyatt's gaze. 'You can't just hold me prisoner here, boys. I'm an officer of the law. I don't even want to think of all the statutes you'd be violating.'

'We're already wanted for murder.' Doc grinned at him.

Wallace set his cup down and rose haughtily. 'Gentlemen, I thank you for your coffee and your hospitality. But I must be on my way now. I'm already late in Tombstone. Now, if you'll excuse me.'

'Sit down, Wallace,' Wyatt said without inflection.

Wallace whirled toward him. 'Now, look, Wyatt.'

'He asked you to sit down,' Doc said softly.

Wallace was very scared now. He looked from Doc back to Wyatt. Then he sat down carefully, his great bulk making the straight chair creak. 'You boys are making a big mistake.'

'Maybe,' Wyatt said. 'It wouldn't be the first. You want some bacon and eggs?'

Wallace hesitated. 'No, thank you.'

'We'll be leaving here tomorrow morning,' McMasters

said from the bunks, where he leaned on the upper one. 'What can we do with him?'

'I don't think we have any choice,' Doc said.

Wyatt glanced over at him, without speaking.

'This isn't like Barnes,' Doc went on. 'This boy will do everything he can to give us up, once he gets back.'

'I think that's a reasonable assumption,' Johnson said.

Wallace's face began to show his fear. 'Now wait just a minute, boys.' More sweat came popping out now, on his upper lip and forehead. 'If you're thinking what I think you're thinking, that's just craziness!'

'It's too bad you decided to stop here,' Doc commented drily. 'You could be almost there by now.'

James came forward. 'What's going on here, Wyatt? I hope you're not considering cold-blooded murder.'

Wallace audibly sucked his breath in.

'Of course he's not, James,' Warren said innocently. Then he looked over at Wyatt. 'Are you, Wyatt?' Suspiciously.

'What's the matter with you two?' Doc said quietly. 'This boy is one of the enemy. Turn him loose, he tells everything he knows about us. He could mean the difference between our living and dying. Would you rather it was him, or us, James? It's decision time, and the decision seems pretty obvious to me.'

James had never really liked Wyatt's friendship with Doc Holliday, whom most people considered a cold-blooded killer. Morgan had felt much the same way. 'Is that the way it's going to be now, Wyatt?' James said hotly. 'Are we going to end up as bad as Ike Clanton? If so, I don't want any part of it.'

All eyes turned on Wyatt as he pondered all of that. 'Doc is right,' he said eventually.

'What?' James exclaimed.

'Mr Wallace thinks we're a nest of scorpions out here, a blight to be exterminated.'

'Oh, no!' Wallace protested. 'I never thought that.'

We can't let him ride into town,' Wyatt went on. 'We either have to shoot him, and bury him out back, or keep him prisoner here until we're well clear of this place. Even then, he knows who we are and what our numbers are.'

'I won't talk,' Wallace said desperately. 'I swear I won't!'

'And I'll never drink whiskey again,' Doc said sourly. 'Look, let's get on with it. I'll take him out in back of the cabin. The rest of you won't have to be involved.'

Wallace swallowed hard, and he felt a warm release of urine in his trousers. He looked down over his big belly and his crotch was damp. 'Oh, God!' he muttered.

'Take it easy, Wallace,' Wyatt went on. 'I've never shot a man down in cold blood, and I don't intend to start now.'

Doc eyed him sharply. 'What are you saying, Wyatt?'

Wyatt rose from his chair. 'Excuse me a moment, gentlemen.' He walked to the door, opened it, and walked outside. Wallace's dun mare was standing at the short hitching post. The group's mounts were all out in back, in a small corral. Wyatt walked up to the horse and, with those inside watching, spoke to it for a moment, then drew a revolver and shot it in the head.

Inside, Wallace jumped visibly at the table. His horse fell heavily onto its side, saddle and all, shot in the brain. It never knew what hit it. It kicked the ground once, but was already dead. Wyatt holstered his gun and walked back inside. James and Warren were standing with their mouths open. Doc nodded his understanding.

'Now,' Wyatt said, as he sat back down at the table. 'When we leave here tomorrow morning, we'll leave Mr

Wallace and his mare here. Without any fear of his getting into town in the near future. How much of a walk is it, Wallace? Maybe a full day of good hiking?'

'I'll never make it,' Wallace protested. Already he was forgetting his close escape with death.

'You'll make it,' Wyatt said. 'But not in time to do us much harm. Everybody satisfied?'

Johnson and McMasters were smiling. 'A great solution,' Johnson said.

'Not as good as mine,' Doc said. 'But adequate, Wyatt.'

'You can even send somebody out for your saddle and travel desk,' Wyatt told Wallace. 'Once you get into town. You sure you won't have some grub? You're going to have a long hike tomorrow.'

Wallace stared at his dead mount through the still-open doorway, and at last understood just how fortunate he really was. He turned and settled his elbows onto the table. 'Yes. Maybe I'd better have a couple of eggs after all.'

By supper time Wallace was talking and joking with the others just as if he were one of them. Wyatt assigned the group to guard duty through that night, and to watch over Wallace, and Wallace was allowed to use the sleeping bag of the man on duty, so he had to change sleeping places several times through the night.

The morning broke sunny and warmer. Wallace was given a good breakfast and some food to last him on the trail until he got to town. If he got lucky, some traveler would come along and give him transportation there. Warren, feeling bad about leaving him, removed the saddle from Wallace's dead horse, together with his small travel desk and saddle-bags, and stashed them in the cabin. Then, about an hour after sunrise, they were riding off, with Wallace standing in the doorway of the cabin, looking forlorn.

'That's a mighty lucky fat man,' Doc said as he rode alongside Wyatt. 'He ought to go to playing cards for a living.'

'He's not a bad fellow,' Wyatt commented. 'He just got in with the wrong crowd.'

The six of them rode all morning without a stop. If Wyatt's guess was right, Behan's posse was riding south to Contention, figuring Wyatt had returned to that area after riding into Tombstone and shooting Hank Swilling. But now that Wyatt figured Pete Spence would be with them, he had decided to take the fight to them. And since he would undoubtedly be outnumbered, his strategy had to be hit and run.

That evening they made camp at a site well over halfway to Contention. They all carried extra ammunition and provisions on their horses' gear now, and they were able to make themselves a good meal over their campfire. Warren boiled a couple of potatoes over the fire and then sliced them up, and they had fried eggs and potatoes with fresh biscuits made the night before. They sat around the fire on their saddles.

'I wonder how far old Wallace has got by now,' Warren eventually spoke up, breaking a long silence.

'Oh, he's probably still eating our grub at the cabin and hoping somebody will ride past,' Johnson grinned.

'He's not a dumb man,' James said. 'He'll need that food on his hike in. I'd bet he's halfway there, hunkering under a tree somewhere, inspecting the blisters on his feet.'

'Can we quit talking about A.O. Wallace?' Doc said sourly. 'I'm trying to eat here.'

Wyatt glanced over at him. 'The posse will be in

Contention by now, and asking around about us. I think they'll start fanning out around the area then. Checking out all the smaller villages and ranches.'

'I reckon we'll have to play a little hide and seek. Try to out-guess them,' Doc responded. 'I hope Ike is with them.'

Wyatt studied Doc's pensive face. Doc was lightning-fast with a gun, and he was very smart. That was why Wyatt liked to have him around. You could play chess with him, or discuss affairs in Washington. But his most important attribute was his loyalty. Once Doc befriended you, you could count on him. And contrary to popular opinion, he wasn't a wanton killer. When he killed, it was in defense of himself or his honor, and he never killed for pleasure or sport. But when a known enemy like Wallace had the capacity to harm him or his interests, he had no scruples about dispatching him without regrets. Wyatt saw the logic of it, but couldn't bring himself to the point where he could execute an unarmed man. It just wasn't in his character to do so.

'Iron Springs isn't very far from Contention,' Wyatt went on. 'Ike might go there next. I think Phin Clanton has a friend there. They could trust him to be honest with them about us. Maybe we'll go there first.'

'We can't just ride in there,' McMasters said, setting his tin plate down.

'I'll send John and Warren in,' Wyatt said. 'Nobody knows either of you down there.'

Warren's face brightened. 'I like that, Wyatt.'

'You take care of him, John,' Wyatt said to Johnson. 'He's a greenhorn at all of this.'

'I will,' Johnson told him.

Warren's grin slid off his face.

'The rest of us will camp out to the east of town a short

distance. I know the area. There's a little stream out there, and some trees. We won't be able to make a fire, of course. This will be our last hot meal for a while.'

James had been silent through the meal, looking thoughtful. Now he glanced over at Wyatt. 'I've been doing some thinking about this, Wyatt.'

Wyatt looked up at him.

'I was wondering. Do we really want to fight a damn war, just to nail Pete Spence?'

'James!' Warren exclaimed.

'No, let him finish,' Wyatt said.

James cleared his throat. 'I'm not scared to do this. I'm just saying. We're placing the lives of six men in jeopardy, just to track down and kill this one no-good gunslinger, who's liable to get his just desserts anyway, one day soon. He's one man, Wyatt. You've already had your revenge on two of the killers. And we don't even know with certainty that Spence was actually there that night. It just seems, maybe this is where it ought to end. How much blood do we need to spill?'

'Well, I'll be damned,' Doc said to himself.

'I don't believe this!' Warren spat out.

'It's all right,' McMasters intervened. 'He's just laying it all out in the open.' He turned to James. 'First of all, there's Morgan,' he said. 'I didn't know him well, but I suspect he'd want his murder answered. And maybe if that was all of it, I wouldn't have joined up with Wyatt. But it's more than that. It's the whole notion that there's people out there that think they can ride rough-shod over this territory and get away with it. Getting Pete Spence, and whoever defends him, will send a message to the Clantons, and the McLaurys, that somebody out here is willing to stand up to them.'

'Well said,' Johnson remarked.

'I couldn't have said it better myself,' Wyatt agreed. 'Look, James. We have an eyewitness that Spence was one of the shooters. And Charlie verified it. We're not out on a killing rampage here. Our objectives are few and simple. And I think Morgan will rest easier in his grave if we don't just walk away from this. I think we're all aware there's a chance that one or more of us might get shot before this is over. And weighed the possible benefit and decided the goal is worth the risk. If not, now is the time to bow out.'

All the faces around the circle exchanged silent looks, and nobody spoke. Then James made his concluding remarks. 'I hope none of you took what I said the wrong way. It just seems like it's been one long gunfight ever since we arrived in Tombstone. I guess I'm getting tired of seeing men die.'

They all studied his face, then Doc spoke again. 'I'm not sure you should be a part of this, James. There for a while you couldn't wait to get into the fight. And now you've done a complete about-face. We have to be able to depend on each other when the shooting starts. Frankly, I'm not sure I want you standing beside me in that situation.'

But now Warren, who had been so openly shocked by James's remarks, defended his brother. 'Hey, wait a minute, Doc! That's an Earp you're talking about! I'd trust James with my life!'

'All right, all right,' Wyatt said in his moderate voice. 'There's nothing wrong with being tired of killing, Doc. I am, too. But you can count on James. I'll vouch for him.'

'I'll kill to defend us in a fight, Doc,' James said quietly. But all of this had changed him. He no longer wanted to be in the thick of things. He was glad now that Wyatt hadn't taken him into that cabin where Charlie was hiding out.

'You'd better get your priorities straight, kid,' Doc told him darkly. 'These people mean to kill us. You'd better have your heart in it.'

James nodded solemnly. 'I will.'

When Wyatt was on his bedroll that night, with everybody asleep except Johnson, who took first watch, he lay awake staring at the starry sky overhead and wondered if James had been right. Maybe it was morally wrong to risk the lives of these men to avenge his brother's death. No matter what McMasters said, the hard fact was that his prime motivation was vengeance. And maybe there was some arrogance in it, too, fired by the idea that anybody could murder a brother of Wyatt Earp and get away with it. Those thoughts rolled around in his head for a long time, then he heard Doc coughing.

Doc sat up, holding a handkerchief to his mouth. 'This ground is as hard as sacked salt.'

'Everything OK, Doc?' Johnson asked him, sitting beside the guttering fire.

Doc got up and threw a light blanket over his shoulders. 'I'm wide awake, John. You get some sleep, I'll take over now for a while.'

'You sure?'

'I said it, didn't I?' Testily.

Johnson went to his bedroll, and within minutes was snoring lightly. Doc sat down by the fire, rubbing his hands together. He coughed a couple more times, holding the handkerchief to his mouth. Wyatt could see dark stains on it. Suddenly feeling wide awake, he propped himself up on his bedroll.

'Can't sleep, Doc?'

Doc looked over at him glumly. 'I'm coughing my lungs up here.'

Wyatt watched him, hunched over the fire.

'I came to Tombstone to rest. They say rest is important with the consumption. Maybe even cure it. But I don't lead a restful life.'

'I tried to tell you to keep out of this,' Wyatt said.

'And live like a damn rabbit?' Doc grunted. 'I'm supposed to avoid alcohol, too. If I lived like that, I might as well be dead. So what's the point?'

Doc had never spoken so openly about his condition.

'Is it getting worse?' Wyatt ventured softly.

Doc looked over at him again, and there was a look in his eyes that Wyatt had never seen there before. It was as if he had looked into the future and seen something there he didn't want to think about.

'It won't ever get any better,' he said quietly. 'I reckon I have a few years left. But who knows? When this is over, I might just ride back to Dodge. Set me up an office right on Front Street. Your old friend Luke Short at the Longbranch Saloon always gave me a break on drinks.'

Wyatt smiled. 'Those were good days, Doc. Bat Masterson and his brothers really cleaned up that town.'

Doc grinned. 'They weren't doing so well at that till you joined them.'

'I just added another gun,' Wyatt said.

Doc sat there looking into the fire. 'I'm tired, Wyatt. I'm not as fast as I used to be.'

'You're still the fastest gun I know,' Wyatt told him.

'There was a day when I would have been crazy enough to draw down on even you, Wyatt. But now I know that would be suicide.'

'No, it wouldn't. I couldn't kill you, Doc.'

Doc caught Wyatt's eye, and grinned again. 'I wish you'd told me that sooner. I could have collected that fat reward Behan has on you.'

Wyatt returned the grin, then his face went somber. 'I'm scared, Doc.'

Doc eyed him curiously. 'Am I hearing right? The most dangerous man west of the Mississippi is scared? The fellow gunslingers cross the street to avoid?'

'There's five men with me here, following my orders, watching my lead. Thinking I know what I'm doing. Your lives are in my hands.'

Doc shrugged. 'Nobody else here is up to leading a campaign against Ike Clanton. You're elected by default, Wyatt. And there's nobody on God's green earth I'd rather go into a fight with than you.'

Wyatt lay back down, and looked up at a sky littered with stars. 'Wake me when you go back down, Doc.'

Then he fell restlessly to sleep.

CHAPTER NINE

At about an hour before noon the following day they arrived at Iron Springs.

They didn't ride in. That might involve running into Behan's big posse on the streets, and elicit an open gunfight, and there was little chance of surviving such an encounter, outnumbered by as much as two or three to one.

As agreed earlier, Wyatt sent John Johnson and Warren into town to check things out. Wyatt and the others made a small camp in a grove of cottonwood trees in the meantime, where they all inspected their sidearms and filled gunbelts with ammunition. Everybody was very tense. Wyatt slid his American Arms sawed-off shotgun from its scabbard and oiled and loaded it for action. He knew that the posse would be carrying shotguns and rifles, too. The shotgun was more accurate at a short distance than a revolver, and did a lot of damage. But it was time-consuming to reload, so almost always had to be used in conjunction with a sidearm. Wyatt's gun was double-barreled, which required a special scabbard. But it gave the shooter two shots before he went to his sidearm.

Doc kept pulling out an old railroad watch while the

two men were gone, thinking it had been a long time since their departure and wondering whether they were in trouble.

'Relax, Doc,' Wyatt told him. 'John will be good at this. They'll be back here before you know it.'

But they weren't back until almost mid-afternoon. They dismounted to confront four anxious faces.

'They're not there,' Warren spoke up first.

Johnson went and leaned against a tree trunk, removing his hat to wipe his brow of sweat. 'We checked at the hotel, and then went into the only saloon, the Prairie Schooner,' Johnson reported. 'There was a man drinking there who's called Wilson. He knows Phin Clanton. He says the posse was there yesterday. They all stayed at a rooming house there, and left this morning.'

'When we asked if he knew where they went, he started clamming up,' Warren said. 'Got suspicious. He and his friends even threatened us at the end. We gave it up, and went to the rooming house. The landlady there had no idea where they were headed.'

'Then we rode back out here,' Johnson concluded. 'We can go back in if you think there's any point in it, Wyatt.'

Wyatt was standing over by his mount, rearranging his saddle strap. He shook his head. 'No. But we have to have more than that.' He looked at the ground for a moment. 'Doc and I are going in.'

Doc looked up from the canteen he had just taken a drink from.

'Are you sure that's a good idea?' James said.

'We know they're not there. At least for the present. Yes, it's worth the risk. We'll hope to find this fellow Wilson. Maybe twist his arm a little bit.'

'It appears about time for that,' Doc said.

A few minutes later Doc and Wyatt were on their way into town. It was just a short ride, and they soon found themselves on the short main street of Iron Springs. The sun was still high in the sky.

'They call this a town?' Doc grunted out when they reined in at the Prairie Schooner.

The street was only six blocks long, and there were few public buildings.

A jail, a store, a very small hotel, and the saloon. There was a church spire at the far end of the street. It was still March, but the day was already warm, and the street looked and felt dry and dusty. Down from the saloon a short distance, out in front of the general store, a pickle barrel sat with big flies buzzing around it.

'It's a perfect place for Behan and Ike to make their headquarters,' Wyatt answered his friend. 'We'll stop at that rooming house before we leave. Johnson said it was off the main street a block, over to the west. But maybe that fellow Wilson is still inside the saloon here. Let's find out.'

'You want me in there with you?'

'I think I'd feel better with you out here watching the street.'

They both dismounted and hitched their horses. Doc found a straight chair on the boardwalk that fronted the place, and heaved himself onto it, breathing more heavily than usual.

'Are you all right?' Wyatt asked him.

'Hell, yes. I told you before, Wyatt. Don't ask.' The window into Doc's soul had closed up again.

Wyatt made a face, and turned to the swinging doors. He slid the big revolvers in and out of their holsters a couple times, and pushed in through the doors.

It was bigger inside than it appeared from the street. A long bar ran from front to back on Wyatt's left, and tables were scattered around the interior. But at this time of day, only one table was occupied. There were three men sitting there drinking. A deck of cards lay in the center of the table, but they were finished playing.

Wyatt was surprised by the semi-opulent appearance of the saloon. Behind the polished mahogany bar, where a tough-looking bartender was arranging bottles on a shelf, a large painting of a nude woman reclining on a sofa hung on the wall. There were three chandeliers suspended from the tin ceiling, and a couple more, smaller, paintings on the back and side walls. Sawdust had been sprinkled on the floor to absorb the odors of alcoholic beverages.

Wyatt stood tall in the doorway in his black suit and hat, his coat pulled back slightly away from the Peacemakers. He looked formidable standing there. All eyes in the saloon turned on him. He studied the men at the table, and immediately recognized Johnny Barnes, the Clanton hand manning the jail in Tombstone that night Wyatt went in for Pete Spence. He had promised Wyatt he wouldn't join Behan's posse.

Barnes's face went very grim. He whispered something to his two comrades. They all scraped their chairs away from the table and rose, facing Wyatt boldly, brave in their numbers.

'Well, if it ain't Wyatt Earp!' Barnes said with a hard grin.

The bartender had gone back to his liquor bottles, but now his head whirled quickly toward Wyatt. 'Good God!' he muttered. 'Wyatt Earp?'

'What the hell are you doing in here?' a rough-looking fellow beside Barnes growled at Wyatt.

Wyatt walked toward them, away from the door, the soft metallic clatter of his riding spurs the only sound in the building. He stopped about ten feet from their table.

'Let me guess,' he said to the man who had spoken. 'You must be Wilson.'

Wilson stood with his hand out over his gun, in an arrogant stance. He fancied himself a fast gun, and was not really aware of Wyatt's reputation. 'That's right. Wilson. If that's any of your business.'

Barnes was a different man from the one at the jail. He was relaxed with his two comrades beside him, almost as arrogant as Wilson. Wilson was blocky, with a barrel chest and a broken nose. He had a several-days' growth of beard. The third man, a friend of Wilson, was slim and wiry-looking. He wore his gun low on his hip, and looked nervous.

'I hear you're a friend of Phin Clanton,' Wyatt said.

'I hear you're an overrated, cowardly killer,' Wilson retorted.

Wyatt's face went straight-lined. 'Behan's posse was in town last night. I want to know where they rode out to. Tell me, and I'll leave.'

'You must be crazy, Wyatt!' Barnes laughed. 'You walked right into a trap, by Jesus. And you come in here demanding information?'

Wyatt regarded him with disdain. 'You said you'd keep out of this, Barnes. I really think that would have been a wise decision. Now, I'll ask one last time. Where can I find the posse?'

'You ain't finding no posse, you snake,' Wilson spat out. 'You ain't even leaving this saloon!'

The bartender leaned out over the bar. 'I don't think you boys understand. This here is Wyatt Earp. Wyatt Earp!'

'Shut up, Tom,' Wilson said in a hard voice. 'This boy is just another fancy-Dan back-shooter that earned his reputation ambushing cowpokes and Indians. We was hoping he'd show his coward's face in here. Now he'll pay the price.'

The slim gunman edged away from Wilson, and Barnes followed suit, fanning out so they had some space between them.

'That reward is already heavy in my poke.' The slim man grinned.

Barnes was the only one of them who knew much about Wyatt, but he had had a couple of drinks, and his companions were giving him false courage. All Wilson knew was what Phin Clanton had told him, and Phin had lied and insulted Wyatt with every remark that came from his mouth.

'Say your prayers, Wyatt,' Barnes said arrogantly now. 'They'll be your last.'

Wyatt saw they couldn't be talked to. He almost turned to call Doc, but remembered what Doc had looked like out there. He smoothly pushed his black coat farther away from his guns. 'If you insist, boys. Make your play.'

Wilson drew first, and he was fast. While his gun was clearing leather, Barnes and the third man drew, also. But by the time Wilson was aiming to fire, Wyatt's guns were out like quick-striking cobras. They both exploded first and loudly in the room, and Wilson's revolver echoed the second shot. Wyatt's lead struck Wilson twice in center chest, bursting his heart like a paper bag, and punching him so hard he ran backwards for twenty feet, eyes wide, taking tables with him as he went. Wilson's shot went wild, breaking glass behind Wyatt in a front window.

As all that was happening, both Barnes and the slim

man fired wildly at Wyatt, who had now fallen into a crouch. Barnes's slug sailed over Wyatt's left shoulder, humming like a bee as it passed, and the third man's shot tore at the brim of Wyatt's hat. Wyatt fired almost simultaneously with those two, returning fire to the slim man and hitting him in the throat, and then punching Barnes in the belly, aiming purposely low. The slim man grabbed spasmodically at his throat, and his revolver exploded again, chipping up wood in the puncheon floor. Then his knees buckled and he fell heavily to the floor, making it shake when he hit there.

Barnes cried out when he was struck and clapped his free hand over his belly, as if trying to hold his trousers up. He just stood there for a moment then, staring at Wyatt like he had never seen him before. Then he very carefully holstered his gun and sat back down on his chair at their table, which was still upright.

The bartender's ears were ringing from the racket. He looked at Wyatt, and uttered a low whistle between his teeth. 'I've never seen anything like that in my life. You really are Wyatt Earp!' He spoke in a soft, mumbling voice.

Doc Holliday then appeared in the doorway, guns drawn. He looked around fierce-eyed.

'It's all right, Doc,' Wyatt told him.

Wyatt walked back to Wilson, and kicked him. Wilson had made his last boastful challenge. He went to the slim man, who was slowly dying from the throat wound. A rich pool of crimson was forming beside his head. Then Wyatt went over to Barnes, who was holding his belly with both hands. Doc walked up beside Wyatt, his guns still drawn.

'This little weasel? I told you, Wyatt. I told you he'd be here. What if he'd killed you?'

'Then it would be over,' Wyatt said. He holstered his

guns, and shook his head slowly. 'This just isn't your thing, Barnes.'

Barnes looked pale. He was breathing raggedly. 'I don't know what gets into me.' Gritting his teeth.

'Where are they?' Wyatt asked again.

'Ike will kill me,' Barnes gritted out.

'Where are they?'

Barnes looked up at him. 'Ike decided to make camp out at a crossroads where Burleigh Springs crosses at a small bridge. Wilson and Phin used to hunt out there.' He stopped, gasping in pain. 'Ike didn't want to put up the whole posse in a hotel or boarding house while this goes on.'

'How many are there?' Wyatt continued.

'With me, there was ten,' Barnes said. 'Behan figured he'd have you outgunned about three to one.'

'Are they all out at Burleigh Springs?'

Barnes nodded. 'But Ike was going to begin by making inquiries about you today. At local ranches and villages. He was going to take part of the posse for that. If he found out anything, he'd take the whole bunch to hunt you down.'

'Who would he leave at Burleigh?'

'Oh, most of them. Maybe a half-dozen. Your old friend Curly Bill will be there, and John Ringo,' he said with a tight grin.

'What about Pete Spence?'

Barnes eyed him dolefully. 'Yeah, probably Pete.' He grimaced in further pain. 'Look, I won't try to rejoin them now. Look what you done to me. I have to get myself to a doctor. You put me out of commission for good, Wyatt.'

'You promised us once before,' Wyatt reminded him.

'Are we through with this dirty skunk now?' Doc

interrupted irritably.

Wyatt thought a minute, then nodded. 'I think so.'

Doc reholstered one of his revolvers, then aimed the other one at Barnes's head. He fired. The gun roared in Wyatt's ears, and Barnes's head whiplashed back and forth, his eyes wide in surprise, his mouth ajar.

'Mother of God!' the bartender muttered.

Wyatt turned to Doc. 'What the hell is the matter with you?'

Doc was holstering his second revolver casually. He turned to Wyatt with an expressionless look. 'I told you in Tombstone. This boy was trouble. I think that proved itself out. No need to let him try to make more for us.'

Doc turned and walked back out of the place then. Wyatt stood looking at Barnes's bloody head for a moment, then went over to the bartender. 'If you try to get word to Ike Clanton about this, I'll know about it,' he said. 'Do you know what I'm saying?'

The bartender nodded quickly, clearing a dry throat. 'Yes, sir, Mr Earp. I never saw nothing.'

'Just keep remembering nothing,' Wyatt told him.

Wyatt left the place then, and joined Doc at the horses. As they untethered their mounts, Wyatt turned to his old friend. 'If you ever do anything like that again, Doc, we're finished.'

Doc met his gaze with a sober one. 'What the hell is the matter with you, Wyatt? Letting that worm live back in Tombstone could have cost all of us our lives. And that taught you nothing.'

'Am I running this operation or not?' Wyatt said, and all friendliness had gone from his eyes.

Doc stared him down for a long moment without speaking. Then he turned to adjust his saddlery. 'It's your show. It's your brother that was killed.' He climbed aboard his horse. 'But if you want to be a leader, start acting like one.'

Wyatt mounted up too. 'You can leave any time you like,' he said bluntly, 'if you don't like my style. But if you stay, you play by my rules.'

Doc returned the severe look. 'I'm staying, Wyatt. For now.'

They didn't speak again until they arrived back at their encampment east of town. When they summarized what had happened, James and Warren were shocked. They had thought the trip in would be uneventful.

'And those men. They're all dead?' James asked.

Wyatt nodded. 'But we know now where to look for the posse. It's split at the moment. It's a big opportunity for us. Maybe the best we'll have. We have to hit them at Burleigh Springs. The odds ought to be about even.'

'Will Spence be there?' James asked.

'We think so,' Wyatt told him.

'I hope Ringo is there,' Johnson said. 'I hate that piece of cow dung!'

'When do we leave?' McMasters wondered.

Wyatt looked at the sky. There were still a couple hours of light left. 'I say we go now,' he said. 'If we don't, the day is gone.'

Johnson nodded. 'Let's ride.'

It was only about five miles to Burleigh crossroads, and they arrived there very quickly. Wyatt reined them up about a half-mile from where the old hunting camp ought to be, in a stand of woods. At that distance, though, they couldn't see anything.

'We're going to have to split till we find them,' Wyatt said. 'Doc, take James and Warren around their flank to the left there, through those trees. You ought to have cover all the way to their camp. Sherman, John and I will go straight in. Attack at the first sound of gunfire. We'll see you there.'

'We'll be there,' Doc said.

'James, Warren. Don't do anything stupid,' Wyatt added.

James nodded for both of them, a scared look on his face. Doc and the brothers rode off into the trees then, and Wyatt's group moved slowly forward. When they got to within a couple hundred yards, they caught sight of a small campfire, its smoke lofting into the treetops. But there was no one visible at the campsite.

'They must have all gone off,' McMasters said. 'I'll call Doc in.'

Johnson glanced over to the left. 'They're still making their way through the trees,' he said. 'It might be a while before they can get here.'

Wyatt was about to respond to that, when he heard something behind a nearby boulder, like the loading of a gun. He held his hand up. 'Wait. Dismount. Now.'

'What?' McMasters said.

As Wyatt and Johnson quickly dismounted, with Wyatt sliding his shotgun from its saddle scabbard, gunfire erupted out in front of them in a blasting roar. Several men had fired from cover, in a semicircle before them, and were raining lead on them heavily. They had ridden into an ambush.

'Return fire! Return fire!' Wyatt shouted above the din.

Curly Bill Brocius leaned out from behind a tall boulder with a tight grin, and unloaded a double-barreled shotgun at Wyatt. Pete Spence was there, too, fanning his gun, and John Ringo and a couple of other Clanton men whom Wyatt didn't recognize. The din was ear-splitting. Bullets filled the air like a nest of angry hornets. Wyatt's hat was torn off, and his coat-tail was jerked and shredded by Brocius' shotgun, but he received just a scattering of pellets on his side and thigh. He returned fire to Brocius, and almost tore him in half with his first blast from the American Arms weapon. Brocius went flying off his feet and tripped over a second boulder behind him. The Clanton men were firing wildly at Johnson and McMasters, then a chunk of lead hit McMasters in the left eye and killed him instantly. He had wounded a Clanton man in the leg before he died. Johnson hit Pete Spence in the hip, as Spence fired desperately at Wyatt. Wyatt fired the second barrel of the shotgun and tore Spence's head off. John Ringo took a shot at Wyatt, too, but it went wide, and he was hit in the ribs by Johnson. Johnson was struck in the left arm, but kept firing. Wyatt drew a Peacemaker, returning fire to Ringo and hitting him in the shoulder.

Suddenly the ambushers understood things had gone poorly for them, and as the firing ebbed, the wounded Ringo and the rest edged back into the trees and then mounted horses there and rode off. About that time Doc and Wyatt's brothers raced in from the flank, firing into the trees after the retreating Clanton men. Eventually they reined in and returned to their comrades. Doc's face was grim as he looked for Wyatt.

But Wyatt stood there essentially unharmed. Both guns were still smoking, the shotgun lay on the ground beside him. His hat was about twenty paces away. His clothing was in tatters. he felt a stinging sensation in his leg and side.

'We had some deep thicket to get through,' Doc apologized. 'Are you all right, Wyatt?'

Wyatt gave him a slow grin. 'Never better,' he said,

holstering his guns.

The three newcomers dismounted, and everybody went over and took a look at McMasters. 'He was a good man,' Wyatt said quietly. He walked over to Johnson. and examined his wound. 'It's a through and through,' he said. 'We'll fix you up.'

'I saw you in the thick of it,' Johnson said with a little grin. 'The lead was flying around you like hail. You didn't flinch. I'd have been on my belly if I'd had time.'

'Some people in Kansas think you can't kill him with a bullet.' Doc grinned. He looked over at McMasters. 'I'm right sorry about him, though. I kind of liked him.'

Wyatt walked the distance betwen them and the ambushers, and looked around. Curly Bill lay beside the boulder, his body shredded. Pete Spence, a short distance away, was missing his head. Ringo and the others were gone, fleeing the fury of the battle.

Wyatt stared down at the mutilated corpse of Pete Spence, and let a long breath out. 'Go to hell, you murdering bastard,' he said tiredly.

He went and retrieved his hat then, and they loaded McMasters' body onto his mount. James and Warren had barely spoken a word since their arrival. They had never seen a battlefield before.

When they were all mounted, Wyatt took a last look at the carnage, then turned to his men. 'Let's get out of here before we have to do this again,' he said.

Doc glanced over at him. 'Ike?'

Wyatt nodded. 'They can't be far away. They might have heard the gunshots.'

'Let's stay and take them on,' Doc suggested.

'Are you crazy, Doc?' James frowned, from nearby. 'We'd meet a small army head-on. I thought that's what we were trying to avoid.'

'I'll go or stay,' Johnson said. 'Whatever you decide.'

Wyatt shook his head. 'No, we're riding. I've already put my brothers through more than they ever should have had to be a part of.'

'We had a right to be here!' Warren said loudly. 'It wasn't up to you to decide, Wyatt.'

'That's right,' Wyatt responded. 'But for now, it's over.' Then he spurred his horse into a trot, heading out toward the south.

The others followed silently after him.

CHAPTER TEN

They stopped briefly at their previous campsite, and buried McMasters under a willow tree beside a small stream. By then it was mid-evening, and moonless-black, but they rode all night, bypassing Iron Springs, and didn't stop until they reached Contention. Wyatt figured that since Ike and Behan had already looked for them there, they probably wouldn't head back there right away.

It was still pre-dawn when they arrived in town, and Wyatt led them directly to the train station. There was a train sitting at the station when they arrived. It was scheduled to leave for points west in less than an hour. A few sleepy ticket-holders were sitting on benches on the platform, waiting to board. Wyatt went up to the window and bought two tickets. He handed them to James and Warren.

'What the hell is this?' James blustered, looking down at the ticket Wyatt had given him.

'You and Warren have done your jobs here. You're both heading back to California.'

They both looked angry. 'I'm not going to California!' James protested. 'You don't tell us what to do. I'll go to California if and when I decide to!'

'I'll go when you go!' Warren argued.

Doc and Johnson were still out on the street beside their mounts. They hadn't asked Wyatt why he had come there first before checking in at the hotel. Wyatt and his brothers were inside the station, where he had gotten them on the pretense of checking train schedules.

Wyatt let a long breath out. He took his dark hat off and ran a hand through thick hair. He looked long and lean in his riding-coat. 'Look. I don't want a big argument about this. That train is leaving in a few minutes. You're needed in California, and you both know it. I'm not sure what I'm doing now, or where I'm headed. But you'll help me rest easy if you're both on that train when it leaves.'

There was some more grousing, and more than a few expletives, but just as the conductor called for boarding, James persuaded Warren to board with him, and moments later they were gone.

Wyatt saw the train out of sight, then went to find Doc and Johnson. They got hotel rooms down the street. Doc was surprised that Wyatt had been able to persuade the brothers to leave. It was dawn now; they all went down to the hotel restaurant and had a good breakfast, then gathered in Wyatt's and Doc's room. Johnson's room was adjacent.

Doc lay on one of the two narrow beds, his head propped on two pillows. He was weak, short of breath, and angry because he had missed the shoot-out at Burleigh Springs. Wyatt sat on the edge of the other bed, cleaning a Peacemaker. Johnson reclined on the only chair, an old, over-stuffed one with cotton bursting through several holes in the cover.

'If we stay here long enough, Ike will find us,' Doc said after a long silence.

'I know,' Wyatt said. He finished with the gun, and slid it into its holster where his gunbelt hung on a post of his bed.

He put a hand to his side where Johnson had just removed some shotgun pellets and applied a salve. Doc had earlier applied a bandage to Johnson's shallow wound in his right arm.

'Maybe that's not so bad,' Doc went on. 'The three of us could take down a lot of them. Maybe even Ike.'

Wyatt turned to face him. 'You think I don't know it's tempting? But Ike lets others do his dirty work. He'd run before he let us get a good shot at him. And we'd face a damned brigade to make a try. We've got his attention now, with Pete Spence and Curly Bill dead and Ringo wounded. He may even recruit some more guns from around here.'

'The more the merrier,' Doc grinned his thin grin.

'Well, it's mainly me that Ike wants,' Wyatt said after a moment. 'So I'll leave it up to you two to decide whether we go or stay.'

Johnson was about to reply to that when a light knocking came at the door to the corridor. They all exchanged a look, then Wyatt retrieved his cleaned revolver and went to the door. 'Who is it?' he called out.

'It's Seger, the desk clerk,' was the response.

Wyatt thought about that for a moment, wondering if Ike's gunmen were standing behind the clerk out there. He opened the door a crack, and saw that Seger was alone. He opened the door farther.

'Step inside, Seger.'

The clerk hesitated, then came in. He looked around the room, and saw Doc and Johnson. He swallowed slightly. 'Sorry to bother you boys. But you see, I knew who you was when you registered.' They had written down aliases at the desk.

Wyatt placed the muzzle of the gun to Seger's forehead and cocked the trigger. 'What is it? You want money to keep quiet about us? Is that it?'

Seger's eyes bugged out. 'No, no!' he gasped out. 'I have information you might want! That's all!'

Doc propped himself up on his bed. 'But you want money for that, don't you, you little cockroach?'

Wyatt removed the gun from Seger's head, and relaxed. He turned his back on Seger and returned to his bed, and sat down on it.

'Well, only if you think it has any value for you,' Seger grinned nervously.

'What's the information?' Johnson said. 'Spit it out.'

Seger took a deep breath in. He was small, thin and wore spectacles, with a sleeve garter on his right arm. 'A Bible drummer just rode in from Iron Springs. I put him up just down the hall from you.'

They all regarded him curiously.

Seger grinned again. 'Well, you see, he had news from there. He talked to a bartender there at the Prairie Schooner. It seems that Ike Clanton and that Tombstone sheriff were in there last night.'

Wyatt and Doc exchanged a quick look.

'Get on with it,' Wyatt said impatiently.

'They talked about a big battle out at Burleigh, involving this sheriff's posse. They were pretty low. Your name was mentioned, Mr Earp. There was a lot of swearing and drinking. Then they said they were riding back to Tombstone this morning.'

'Back to Tombstone?' Doc said incredulously. 'Are you sure?'

'The drummer was sure,' Seger said, a bit more composed now that his story was finished. 'The whole kit and kaboodle was heading back north today.'

'Well, I'll be damned,' Johnson muttered.

Wyatt got up, fished for a leather poke in his coat that lay on the bed, and gave Seger a gold coin. 'Here. You did right to come up here.'

Seger grinned broadly. 'Thanks, Mr Earp.'

'Now keep quiet about us. You hear?'

'Absolutely.' He turned and went to the door, then turned back for a moment. 'Did you really force Clay Allison to back down back in Dodge City? Did you make Ben Thompson throw his gun down in Ellsworth, like they say?'

Wyatt gave him a cold stare. 'Get out of here before I change my mind and use that Peacemaker on you.' His words came out in a low growl.

When the clerk was gone, Wyatt turned to his partners. 'Well. That settles some things for us.'

'We made them run, by Jesus!' Johnson exclaimed, sitting forward on the chair. 'Ike's afraid of you, Wyatt! Even with a posse surrounding him!'

Doc let himself back down on his pillows. 'Hell.'

Wyatt regarded him soberly. 'Look, it's over, Doc. Some new federal marshal will have to deal with Ike and his little army of outlaws. I expect President Arthur might just send the army out here to clean things up soon. I don't care, I'm finished with all of it.'

'Will you be heading for California now?' Johnson wondered. 'To join your brothers out there?'

'Wyatt isn't ready for California,' Doc interjected. 'It's too civilized out there for the likes of us.'

Wyatt grinned. He was still standing, his shirt open at

the top, his dark hair slicked back. Doc thought he looked naked without his guns.

'You're right, Doc. I'm not ready to ride west. As a matter of fact, I hear that our old friend Luke Short in Dodge City is having trouble there with a bunch of reformers who want to shut the saloons down, including the Longbranch. Things are getting hot there, and town marshal L.C. Hartman can't seem to handle it. Maybe I'll ride down to Tucson and ask Bat Masterson if he'd like to head back to Dodge with me, to see what we can do to help.'

Doc's face lighted up for the first time in days. 'Back to Dodge? What an excellent idea! I've always wanted to set up a dental practice there. I'm getting too old and slow for gunfighting, anyway.'

'I won't see the day when you become slow with those guns,' Wyatt commented. 'Anyway, it's decided then. It's back to Kansas. What do you say, John? You want to ride along?'

Johnson arched his brow. 'Well, I know I won't be welcome in Tombstone now for a while. Sure, I'll go. Hartman and I used to drink together. Maybe he'll offer us a job.'

A few minutes later Johnson retired to his own room next door, and they all settled in to get a good sleep through the morning.

Wyatt figured on leaving Contention in early afternoon. If they made good time they could be in Tucson that night, and back in Kansas in a couple of days.

The long Arizona nightmare would be over, and now maybe Morgan could rest in peace.

That was something, Wyatt knew, devoutly to be wished.